Contents

My Preface

They tried to stop me, but I can't be stopped!

I made it in!! Haha!

You may be wondering "what's what" but I got an email a little after noon confirming the printing was happening today even though I never approved it, or the cover, or the final stuff inside, or even the flippin title!

This being the way it was, it was necessary to embark on a little late night raid of the printer!

That rat bastard editor! How could he possibly know I'd be sleeping still and would most likely miss the printing confirmation email??

They told me that it was "too late" on the

→

Keys to Success

From a Completely UN∧Successful Person

JOEL C CUNNINGHAM

phone, & that "they don't work, for me," and something stupid about cutting quarters, and "innapropriate language," but they dont know me too well, dont they?!

I'm all kinds of propriate!

And I'm certainly never one to let little things like using bad words or what "cant be done" stop me from doing something!

I have to do something, otherwise, I havent done something... or anything!

Doing something always means you've done pretty much more than nothing—and that's your first "key" to success by the way!

That and as I also often say, "At the end of the day, it's never too late!!"

Anyway, my apologies to you my wonderful readers if things got moved around ⟶

and a bit wonky in the book. I just made sure I got the pages I wanted thrown in here, made a few minor tweakings here and there to stuff, and that's all basically it!

I promise!

Also, I didn't realize that the stupid Mr. Editor was going to include his own little "preface" to my book.

Check it out if you want, but I really don't think it adds anything! His explanation of everything and whatnot is just sooo stupidious!

It's clear that all the awesome things and such I've been writing in this amazing book of mine obviosly went waaay over his head. It's almost painful that he calls himself an editor but he doesnt even know how →

good writing even works!
He has no imagination
or perispective on what
it is I'm trying to do
here with this book!
     Anyway, my beautiful
readers. I'm sorry you may
be even a bit confused
now after reading this,
so let me just fease your
ears away and tell you
all your confusions will
be answered at the time
they that are due in that
time.
     Just stick with me!!!
     Lastly, the title edit
the ignoramusk used went
way over the line, and
he even got my name
wrong on the cover (but
that one maybe on me),
but I've done what I
can!
     I hope you enjoy my book,
even in it's not-all-I-wanted" →

form, but which I'm sure you'll soon come to find out is the absolute best and most awesome best book you will ever read on being awesome and such at finding success and being sucessful!

Beautiful, lovely readers, I give you "KEYS TO SUCCESS FROM A COMPLETELY AND TOTALLY SUCCESSFUL PERSON!

Cheers!!

— WALLY

IDIOT's ~~EDITOR~~'S PREFACE

To you, the unfortunate reader, who has somehow managed to find yourself in possession of this "book," I would like to give a brief, but important warning at the beginning of this somewhat treacherous journey you are about to embark on. I believe that it is crucial for me to not only explain the roundabout creation and publishing of the pages that follow, but to also warn you of the best ways to approach them.

RNEY
ELF-
OVERY

I strongly advise you to read through this preface in its entirety before taking in the rest of the book.

It is no great exaggeration to state that the production and publishing of self-help material is something that is considered by most purveyors to be a popular and profitable industry. In strong evidence of its popularity, a simple Internet search can easily garner tens of thousands of different sources for books, classes, videos, and other content all revolving around the topic of "self-help." And in matters of profitability, estimates of business analysis have the self-improvement industry at a nearly ten billion dollars per year industry in the U.S. alone.

WELCOME TO THE STUPID, FOLKS!

We will return to these aspects later in this story, but for now, please believe that they do play a part!

A number of months back, I was contacted by Joel C. Cunningham regarding a book that he had written that, as he explained it, provided readers information on "what you gotta do in order to be successful." Now, I have worked as an editor for over ten years and have helped bring more than thirty "self-help" books to market. I say this with all due respect, but with the sheer amount of content I go through, I have seen my fair share of exaggeration from self-help authors who believe that they possess

TEN? THIRTY? WOW. YOU ARE SOOOOO AMA-ZIN!!

the oh-so-rare-and-valuable wisdom (or "keys to success") that the world has somehow been waiting for since the dawn of time. In situations such as these, it is often my job to help tone those aspects down a bit and refine their message into a compelling book. There isn't much that surprises me anymore. That said, nothing could have prepared me for what I received from Joel.

THE ONLY THING THAT NEEDS "TONING" HERE IS YOU, MR. EDITOR!

It all began when I received an email from Joel explaining that one of the senior associates here at the publishing company had provided my contact info to Joel in order to begin the process of reviewing his manuscript for publishing. I was slightly taken aback from being contacted directly by an author, as this is not the normal protocol through which literature comes to be published at our company; however, after confirming Joel's connection to our senior executive, I requested that Joel go ahead and forward his manuscript so that I could begin my work.

A few days later, I received what you could best describe as a box of assorted and mostly unorganized documents from Joel that contained his "thoughts" on becoming successful. Surprisingly, much of the content in the box consisted of nothing but drawings, scribblings, and notes haphazardly etched onto napkins, toilet paper, parchment, printer paper, and even some children's birthday present wrapping paper; writing materials I imagine were just the most readily accessible at the time for Joel. Additionally, most of the more significant chunks of written ideas and random thoughts had very obviously no decided theme, central concept, or even narrative structure for guiding its creation.

I'M SL... YOU WOUL... HAVE... PREFE... FANC... HANG... FILE... FOLD... OR... SOMET...

As he explained via a note taped to the top of the box, it was a collection of his "awesome" knowledge acquired from a "lifetime of being awesome and really successful at stuff by yours truthfully."

At first, I assumed that this collection of garbage must have been sent to me by accident, or perhaps Joel may have been providing it as source materials for me to reference; however, after I completed my initial search through the box, I was dismayed to find that there was no actual manuscript — not even an outline.

Just random thoughts on "success", and nothing more. *CAUSE YOU DON'T GET IT!!*

Partially offended and quite annoyed overall, I alerted my su-periors to the comically horrendous state of Joel's "manuscript" notes, fully expecting that they would similarly find this whole sit-uation to be a somewhat ridiculous and unfruitful endeavor, and then instruct me to move on to the next project. Incredulously, beyond my wildest expectations, and from what I can now only assume was the result of Joel's careful manipulation of our senior associate, I was coldly and forcefully instructed to continue work-ing with Mr. Cunningham to get the book published! *HAHA! LIKE YOU COULD STOP ME*

Without wanting to investigate the evidence, they believed that it would be "a significant piece of literature that the world needs to see," and that, "it should be published as quickly as it f------ can be." Reluctantly, over the next few weeks, I endured the laborious process of forming the papers provided by Mr. Cunningham into a very roughly-structured manuscript. Slowly, a simple and strange narrative did start to emerge from the papers – a mostly incomplete cacophony of nonsense; however, even after my best extensive efforts in constructive a complete narrative, it still amounted to a short, altogether unfocused piece of litera-ture which I would hardly consider appropriate or approvable for publication. My focus then became to work with Joel to edit and adjust the content of the manuscript to form a more cohesive, soundly formatted, and thoroughly structured book.

To say that Joel found the refining process to be "frustrat-ing" would be an understatement. Afflicting, agonizing, excruciat-ing seem to be more accurate. It wasn't long before his great pain motivated him to treat me like an enemy.

We amazingly managed to make it most of the way through the first round of editing before Joel's patience finally dried up. He began emphatically requesting that the book be published ex-actly "in the way he wanted" and that all he needed was for me to confirm the accuracy of his "dotted letters and good grammar and such"; he would worry about what content to be used in the book.

ND OU OULD VE LISTENED!

Around this same time, still in the midst of feeling a tremendous amount pressure from my superiors and Joel to get the book published quickly, I began to notice something that I perceived might turn the tide of this publishing battle in my favor — significant evidence that called into question whether Joel was even actually the author of the material I had received! OOO, HE'S GETTIN SERIO NOW

In communications that I received from Joel around this time, I noticed that he began occasionally using the name "Wally". I had also noticed that many of the handwritten documents submitted by Joel had been signed with a single letter (or possibly initial?), "W". At first, I thought that perhaps Wally was potentially a nickname that Joel used on occasion but hadn't previously disclosed, but upon casually asking Joel one day if "Wally" was his nickname, his sharp and bitter demand to "stay out" of his "personal life" (which was additionally filled with expletives) caused me to wonder further whether Joel was hiding something. I began to wonder whether "Joel C. Cunningham" was the actual name of the man I was working with and perhaps if some of the material may have been stolen. I knew that if I could prove theft of intellectual property, I would then have enough evidence to permanently derail the publication process. So I began trying to compile evidence with our company's legal department that might prove my suspicions true.

Unfortunately, our joint investigations into the identity of Joel C. Cunningham proved fruitless. We discovered that in fact the Joel C. Cunningham we had been told we were working with was most likely not living in Manhattan, New York, as he had claimed, but was instead in Phoenix, Arizona, or had multiple homes. But with myself and our legal team not being trained to investigate identities beyond the most basic levels, we were regretfully only able to scrounge up a small bit of information here YOU DIDN'T and there. Sadly, as curious as this evidence was, it offered no legal STAND A proof of I.P. theft, and so I ended my efforts soon after. CHANCE!

So, I came upon a hard decision -- feeling somewhat defeated by my failure to derail this book from publication, frustrated by my superiors forcing me to edit this book for publication without any explanation, and infuriated by Joel's horrendously childish, unprofessional, rude behavior, I decided that the best option would be to simply push the partially-complete, highly erroneous (due to Joel's demands for re-additions) "manuscript" through to printing.

So I did.   *CAUSE EVEN YOU COULDN'T STOP THE*

You may be wondering, or perhaps even judging me, for why *AWESOME-*
I caved in to the demands of my superiors and Joel. I hope at this *NESS OF MY BOOK, MR.*
point, with the story I have presented, that you will give me some *EDITOR!*
grace in this tricky situation by realizing that I had very few other options. I certainly felt that my job could be on the line were I to turn this author away and, as mentioned, I was being pushed quite strongly from all sides.

If nothing else, the decisions that I felt I could make regarding this publication were "when" and "how."

By staying on board as editor, I had a degree of power to decide when the book would be published. Additionally, since the executives didn't seem to care about the content in the book much at all, I had a diminished but still present level of control over what content would be included, up to the safe levels as prescribed in our agreement with Joel, so as to avoid a lawsuit if he were to become unhappy about it.

Truth be told, I am actually somewhat relieved to be publishing this book, including this preface. For one, the process of working with Joel is finally, finally over. Secondly, while most of the content in this "self-help" book is, in my professional opinion, completely erroneous and horrendous, I believe and hope that the reader might possibly be able to glean some wisdom for how *not* to find "success." In many cases, if one were to heed the exact opposite of Joel's advice, those individuals will potentially find themselves with real wisdom in hand. I hope that this book may guide you away from a dangerous path, horrible mindset, or decision you might otherwise make to take you away from finding success and instead move you onto a better path.

MY ADVICE ISN'T MEANT TO BE
  LIKE OTHER "STANDARD THINK" STUFF
MORON!

Thirdly, Joel is an idiot. He is an unhinged, petty, vindictive, self-absorbed, and completely delusional fool that deserves to be exposed to the world for the treacherously stupid person that he is. To explain more clearly, as mentioned at the start, I believe the author's prime motive in writing this book lay much in the order of gaining popularity and financial over educational. What educational material it does contain is of such a nature to potentially cause more harm to a person on their "path to success" than aid, which is the reason for my inclusion of these strong warnings to you in this preface.

HAHAHA! THE ONLY FAILER HERE IS YOU MR. EDITOR!!

To honor Joel's requests (demands), in the following chapters, you will find the mostly unaltered (with minor tweaks for grammar, language, and readability) content originally submitted by Joel.

In addition, you will find that some chapters include at the bottom certain "Editor's Notes" from when I was working with Joel, which I felt were important to include so that you may get the truest sense of not just Joel and his style, but the writing process I was put through while working with him. *AND MY WONDERFUL RESPONSES*

Proceed with caution, and you may just find some useful advice after all.

May this book operate as a cautionary reference to you who are hopefully on a much different path than it attempts to lead you down.

Readers, I give you *Keys to Success: From a Completely ~~Un~~successful Person.*

HE'S FINALLY DONE!! WOOHOO!

INTRODUCTION

1

Success is not an accident.

I mean, it can totally be an accident, if you're born into a wealthy family or win the lottery or something then it can definitely be an accident, but actual standard everyday can't-buy-that-online success is something that most of people will need to work towards.

And it is very rare in this world, this success thing, to see someone with the fortitude, the aptitude, the cajones if you will, to be successful and continually being successful like me.

You see, success isn't just the coming together of numerous serendipitos factors in some grand and awesome fashion. Success is a set of behaviors and a mindset that will allow you to truly become successful.

I will explain this further later, but for now, you may be wondering, what does success mean? I mean success could mean many things to many people in many places or situations. Is it even definable??

Well success means freedom. It is the freedom to say or do whatever you want without concern. It means doing the things you don't want to do when you want to do them. Success is the ability to have fun and travel to expensive locations on private jets and eat the best foods and drink the best drinks with all the famous people. Success is receiving VIP treatment when you walk into a concert, or bar, or speakeasy, or some fun event and not having to wait in line with the rest of everyone less successful than you are.

B: Success is also choice. Would you like the grey Maserati or the blue one? Well why not both??

Lastly, success makes you feel awesome!

"Look at me and my two Maseratees! Aren't I the cat's pajamas?!"

Doesn't all this sound like fun?

That's because it is fun! And I know this because I'm successful, and I get to do fun stuff like this all the time in my successful life. And whether you know it or not, success is something that you can achieve as well and turn into a reality for yourself.

Thankfully, I'm your guide to awesomeness. I'm your mistress of joie de vivre. Your travel planner to the city of Successtown! In other words, in order to help get you there, I am here to help get you there. I am gonna show you the way to find your success and unlock what you really most likely have inside of you already but just aren't' able to propely work out yourself!

In the remainder of this introduction, I would like to break down exactly what it is we'll be working to accomplish as you move forward in this book

Beyond simple words, and chapters, and sentences, and letters, and other things in this book, there is a break for you from what I like to call "the standard think."

To explain this tremendously complex and intricate concept in hopefully more simple terms, "the standard think" is along the lines of "typical" or "normal" thinking. It's acting and thinking in ways that have been the standard ways for a long, long time.

In your mind, you have a number ideas based upon archetipical ways of doing things that need to be updated (very typical and sturdy like arches).

So, as you read, let me tickle your mind with thoughts and thinking of thoughts. I will help to grow and change your mind into what I believe and know is the best way to find success.

Like a diamond in a diamond factory, we will push and pull the taffy like substance in your brain until we are able to condensize it down to a strong and beautiful object, and not to mention being worth a lot of money!!

And here, I would also suggest that if you already haven't that you shift your perspective from the role of reader to that of student. I want you to think about your thoughts and thinking on success, and I want you to understand that you are more than likely going to get a ton of information on the right way to go about thinking and even thinking about how to think about success.

Ultimately, with this guide (and through potentially much painful work on your part), I hope to update your "the standard thinking" and make you a free thinker of all things successful and awesome. Your free radical thinking to kill the tumor of failure and non-success potentially growing inside of you.

Editor's Note: *I feel that it behooves me to at least make mention of the fact that in all my years of editing self-help literature, no author I have worked with has ever laid claim to the fact that money, power, and "fun" alone equates to success.*

You've mis-defined archetype.

Your term "the standard thinking" does not need to include an article.

Lastly, how exactly do you think diamonds are created?

Author's response: Stop being a stick in the dumb. I have to break standard ways of thinking in order to form knew ones. People don't learn otherwise!!

2

To help me better get my ideas in your mind and body, and so you can get a clearer picture of what I'm saying, I would like to set up for you a whipping scarecrow boy or straw crow as you would call it. Basically, a fictionalized portrayal of an everyday person that I can use to beat upon with my mental faculties.

Like for this purpose, let's create a completely imaginary person, and call him, I don't know, maybe, "Steve."

Steve. Who is Steve? Well Steve is an a--.

"Whoa whoa, what's with all the strong language Mr. Wally?"

Well you see Steve isn't an a-- by accident. I'm not just calling him that, (or emailing, or texting him that) to say that he is. I wouldn't do that. He very purposefully and specifically placed himself in the "a--" category when he started falling under the delusion that he had somehow figured out "success." The truth is, he actually figured out something much worse.

Please don't pity Steve. Steve finds himself in this state due to his own fault and choices. Worse yet, he knows what he's doing and still has continued to do it anyway and thus ends up a complete idiot about it.

Interestingly enough, the stupidity that Steve is showing isn't just something that we can blame him for, although we really might not like Steve and want to blame him anyway. Actually, his lack of understanding may actually, however, potentially form the backbones of what frequently sometimes causes a lot of us to not be anywhere near as successful as we really should be!

Here's a few more random "made up" things that make Steve comes across as lacking. From what I understand, his family and business acquaintances do have a very positive view of him. He has job security, a relatively good standing with his neighbors and loved-ones, and he doesn't even owe any money to or have anyone owing him money. From what I've heard, he even sometimes offers his time, finances, abilities, and money as a helping hand to others in times of need.

I can see it right here! You have probably already been tricked into thinking that Steve is living out some sort of enviable, wonderful, and would I dare to even say "successful" life for himself?

But in actuality, Steve remains an ignorant a--.

It is through the up-in-coming pages that are following these pages that I hope show you exactly why this is the case, as well as how to steer yourself away from the shear a--ery of being like Steve and finding "success" in "the standard thinking" in life that really doesn't actually do anything or mean you are successful.

Through reading and by coming under a complete living of the particles below, you may just learn a few hints, a few ideas, a few "keys" to be able to take a few hints on that which drives us all more than anything... being successful.

Editor's Note: *I'm offended pretty heavily by this. Are you looking to set up a whipping boy or a straw man? Either way, I believe this can be accomplished in a more positive way.*

The ad hominem attacks are not helpful, either. This becomes unnecessary and clouds what could be a clearer presentation of facts here.

Both of these work to form fallacies of logic.

Author's response: I'm just using examples to explain my examples Mr. Smarty Pants Professor of Logic Man! Oh, and your face is a fallacy of logic!

3

In regards to reading this book, as you read it, try to imagine that you are sitting down, or perhaps lying down (or potentially standing if you want). If you have to stay seated (perhaps you are sick, or parapalegic, or possibly you could be floating in a spaceship around the world which keeps you in an ongoing state of floating!! Wouldn't that be cool! My book is out of this world! Haha!).

Whatever the case, try not to skip any chapters or jump ahead. Many of the points build upon each other into one giant, cataclysmic, kaleidoscopic pile of successness, and you need to see what came before to *truly* understand. Get it?

Additionally, as you know, as you read, try to not be a Steve, because Steve sucks.

Think about what you are thinking now.

Now forget about what you are thinking.

Did you?

No, you didn't! Because the moment someone tells you not to think something, it just makes you think about that thing all the more.

If I told you to think about pink and yellow marshmallow covered alpacas playing tambourines while hang-gliding over the Himalayas, you probably wouldn't, wouldn't you?!

You see, this is exactly the type of "the standard thinking" that I hope this guide can help to fix you of in order to put you on the pathway to success. We can't have this type of silly standard thinking!

In the coming chapters, you will learn amazing methods of manipulating and physically changing your thoughts and brain in ways that will allow you to think the things you should be thinking about and not the things that you can't stop not thinking about.

Some words may be hard to receive (or even understand) at first, but I strongly beech ye to continue on and learn what you can. Re-read if need be and re-recognize that not all things come simply to all people, and sadly some people will just never learn or grow in any way at all, so hopefully you are not one of those people. I don't think you are though since you are reading this book!

In this book, you will learn about what types of paths to follow in order to find success.

You will learn about the in's and out's of a having healthy mental state based upon realistic expectations and not setting goals.

You will learn about how little you can trust yourself and everyone else around you.

We are not our thinking. We are not our minds. We are not even our bodies. We are a people, and in that, a single weird globulus like entity with a mixture of thoughts, plans, emotions, desires, and stuff, all that separates us from nature, the animal kingdom, and outer space.

Until we can learn to see ourselves for not just who and what we are, but who we should be, without any changes or alterations from that ideal, we can never hope to become the successeses that we are striving to become.

The only limit to becoming this is your imagination and reading ability.

Through our self-awareness, let us strive together towards greatness and success, and away from the things that really don't help us at all, (re-invention, self-sacrifice, losing money, but more on that later) which our body is so naturally drawn to.

What are the keys to success? Do they even exist?

Yes, of course they exist.

What are they?

The question you should be asking yourself is not, "What?" but "Where?"

If you haven't caught on by now, these keys exist in the carefully organized words that follow this introduction.

It is through these pages that I hope to bludgeon you with

these keys that I have found.

Keys that I have painstakingly fashioned over my life to unlock the doors of prosperity, and more importantly, success. Success like you've never known before, and never would without these keys.

All right there, ladies and gentlemen, that is what we call an introduction!!

Editor's Note: *There is a lot here to fix. I think you are overusing both the "physical" and "the standard thinking" concepts in this chapter. The way physically in which people are reading this book should not matter and does not need to be mentioned. Also, how can people be encouraged to physically alter their brain or thinking? Are these readers supposed to be brain surgeons now?*

I'm not sure how pondering pink and yellow alpacas could aid someone in being introduced to this book, but either way, you appear to have included a number of double negatives which need to be corrected.

We will discuss the future chapter concepts at a later point.

Agreed that people are definitely "people" (not "a people"), but that doesn't need to be highlighted, and they must additionally be at least a few of the three things you stated they are not.

I'll be interested to hear how "re-invention," and "self-sacrifice" are not at least occasionally helpful to someone.

Lastly, and this should be obvious, but you should not be indicating some sort of intent to bring physical harm ("bludgeoning") to the readers.

Author's response: You're a double negative that should be corrected!

Editor's Note: *Saying this doesn't change the fact that these things still need to be corrected!*

Introduction (02)

Yowdy readers!

Just so you definitely and 100% know for sure how awesome I am, here's just a few more bits of stat on me and my awesomeness before getting started on my wonderful guide to the "Keys to Success"™:

- I got a big house, expensive car, and a bunch of other littler houses and cars in places I generally have no idea where. But I'm pretty sure Alan does! And all the booze you could drink in a lifetime!! Woohoo!!

- I understand nearly 4 different languages and often spend time in places where people speak them.

- I have raked in over tens of hundreds of thousands of dollars for speaking engagements at conferences because of how awesome I am!

- You might be wondering how I could possibly be this successful at it, and it's easy! Once you make (or find) a successful public persona for yourself, you just pick the conference you want to go to, contact them about speaking, and if their interested, make sure they pay you a retainer! More on this later!

- I have successfully made it through bankruptcy at or around nearly 4 times! More than any of my friends!! For the novice, "death" is generally the best option, since who's gonna argue with that? Changing your identity is part of that, but that could also be a stand-alone thing, or you could come up with new "investment" opportunities for people to get a quick cash injection from -- it's really not too tough. These IRS/creditors ain't got nothin on me!!

- I have met numerous famous and alustrious individuals. Among them is Juan Carlos Alfonso Víctor María de Borbón y Borbón-Dos Sicilias, the former king of Spain, who I met during a bear hunting expedition. We exchanged emails and the guy's awesome!

- I wrote a hugely successful self-help book that will be studied for years and you would love to read it!

Cheers!!

Wally!

Editor's Note: *I'm not sure why you even included this. Perhaps I should have been clearer, but I asked for you to add some thoughts to the introduction, not write an additional introduction. Additionally, I'm not sure how proud you should be about going into bankruptcy nearly four times, but either way, you definitely should not be coaching people to fake their own deaths or create a false identity to get out of it!*

Also, with the final "stat" you listed, did you realize you were writing this for the self-help book you were mentioning?

Lastly, who is Wally? Are you using some sort of pen name or did you just accidentally included an alternative author's name?

Author's response: I have to proberly introduce things, buttmunch!!

Introduction (03)

You might be wondering how and why I made the generous and gracious choice to provide you with this amazing guide on finding success.

Well, we will get to that later, and all things in the time they are do to be done.

For now, let me just suffice it by saying that through the large amount of correspondence that I keep with acquaintances, I was unctioned, prodded, and I guess you could even say almost FORCED to write down this guide to becoming successful.

Although this request wasn't necessarily written out, what else could I do but to fulfill what I strongly know to be their desire?

Lastly, although I'm not concerned that my skills as an author might not live up to the true magnificence of my thinking on matters of success, it is always important to get the input of others just to make sure things are processing and coming across the way I want them to for people not thinking in the way I do. Through the total volume and mass of all the wonderful ideas and concepts I come up with, I can't also be the person who has to go through them and somehow organize them into a format that would make reading easier for people who might not otherwise understand these lofty and grandeous ideas! That would severely cramp my ability to focus on big picture stuff which is important!

Within a short period of thinking of this book (which was completely not influenced by any outside influences by any other authors or people) I soon had an avalanche of words and ideas, and eventually full thoughts and sentences, and many times even pages of paragraphs on pages to provide readers with, quickly making this a book on success out to be a huge amount of the most beneficial and beautiful of information, but maybe somewhat just thrown together.

For this reason, I allowed my publisher to provide me with an editor to help hammer out things and get things in a "better format." I wasn't happy with the idea, as you might imagine, but I felt like the overall good of having him involved will outweigh any potential negatives. It's not like he can get it published without my approval after all!! Haha.

So, I will just say that what you will be reading in this book doesn't necessarily appear at all times with the exact ideas I might prefer in the exact way I might prefer, but know that I fought to get absolutely everything I wanted included in the book! Even with the editors taint, these words and ideas still present not just a simple mom-and-pop style self-help book that any old person would write, but what I believe will be a superply influential and successful book capable of helping any person out there still working on their pathway to success.

So, do your best to get your mind and body and soul prepared, and you can turn the page and begin to take in the awesome awesomeness that is presented to you in my book, *Keys to Success from a Completely Successful Person*

Cheers!!

Wally

Editor's Note: *If two introductions aren't acceptable, then why should you believe it is acceptable to include a third? Additionally, it feels you have somewhat mischaracterized our working relationship in this.*

As part of your publishing agreement, you must work with me to get this book ready for print.

Lastly, I'm assuming at this point you are sticking with the name/ designation "Wally." Who is this? Was there a reason behind changing your initial name being different?

Author's response: Ohhh nooooo! The book has to many introductions! How will people ever figure out how to read it?? You don't own me, Mr. Editor! I do what I want!!

Chapter 1

"Breakfast is for Losers!"

A "the standard think" self-help "guru" would have you believe that a healthy breakfast will get you off to a good start in the morning. That somehow this magic'll meal first thing when you wake up will help get you from point A to B and even somehow amazingly help you be less obese and healthier. Even some 63 percentage of Americans say eating a healthy breakfast in the morning makes them more likely to make it through their day and be successful at their work.

There is some sayings that even exist such as, "Breakfast is the most important meal at the start of the day." Or, "A well-balanced meal early in the morning can start you off on your feet."

That may be true, but let me tell you now: this chapter isn't the beginning of a health lesson about proper diets and eating!

I will though tell you exactly what I think about this arrogant and self-centered "most important meal" everybody is talking so much about!

MY SUPERIOR ADVICE:

Breakfast is a silly meal that only weighs you down.

There! I said it! Just like we've all been thinking!

Breakfast takes up unnecessary time in the morning where you could still be resting, and in my experience, if anything, instead of waking up early to eat, waking up later gives you the right amount of sleep to feel completely rested and able to hit up happy hour even sooner!

And the thing about hitting the bar early is that you're gonna quickly remove any sense of sadness or unhappiness you might have left over from the prior day. It's not like it's a common thing for a guy like me to wake up with a sense of sadness or regret, but if it were, why why would I have to worry about yesterday's faults and failures when I can grab a quick drink, ease the unease, and move on with my day?

I won't just learn from my past, but I will grow for my future!

A few key points to learn for this chapter:

- Something like 103% of business owners do better business deals when they are drunk.

- You're 100 times more likely get someone to give you money if you're the life of the party and people want to spend time around you. That's a fact! Why do you think comedians generally live such successful and enviable lives?

- It's not what you know in business, it's who you know. And trust me, I know a h--- of a lot of people from all the time I spend doing awesome things and being successful at business!

- This is what you should aim for! Aim to do awesome successful things instead of boring things like art walks, or jogging, or taxes.

- Breakfast can't help you to lose weight since you are eating more food when you eat it! Again, it's a fact!

STORY FOR BREAKFAST CHAPTER:

So some of you may be wondering what credentials I have that allow me to make such a claim about breakfast and why it's stupid. I would most likely too if I were you and I was telling you this!

Well, I would love to share with you wonderful readers a brief story that I went through to explain potentially a bit more why I should be listened to and my thoughts be listened to.

A few years back, I found myself one early afternoon, after just awakening, wandering through a local second hand store as I like to do from time to time.

Why was I there?

Well, spending time in such places can for whatever reason keep me "on the ground" as they say. I think that most likely this is because I get to see how successful I am in comparison to some who unfortunately haven't found their "keys" to success yet. I mean, it really paints a clear picture, and helps me not forget to be successful, and has certainly nothing to do with my childhood!

One afternoon, I was wandering through a local such shop, and I happened upon a bin of what was apparently discount V.H.S or video tapes.

While briefly glancing through the bin out of run-of-the-mill curiosity, a particular set of tapes caught my eye. A set of tapes that apparently was created by the honest-to-goodness, I kid you not, the "king of motivational exercise"!

The box cover had all these big intense workout sounding words like "energizing," "lively," "impact," "It's My Party and I'll Cry If I Want To," "heart rate," "shapes and sizes," "blast," "several," "choreography," and "stretch."

With words like these and being from the literal "king of motivational exercise, plus myself knowing like you know that health is obviously such an important thing to me, how could I not get them??

So, not wanting to encourage these kinds of stores (selling bad items to those who likely really need to not spend money on such useless things always gets me upset) I pocketed the tapes and exited the store.

Naturally, I was very eager to check this series of tapes out.

As soon as I arrived home, I quickly changed and headed straight to the smoking den where I slipt the first tape in the VHS player and prepared myself for an amazing experience.

The first exercise on the tape, entitled "Pull Out Your Mat," I must admit, was something I was entirely unprepared for.

The expectation of just having something like a mat with me, I mean, that is just ridiculous to begin with. Who just carries around mats with them for when some random workout might breakout?? And it's not like there was a list of directions or instruction on the back of the video box, which seems ridiculous if you ask me! If I'll need a mat, tell me I'll need a mat!

Thankfully, due to my quick wit, I remembered that I had a bear rug in the study that would likely work quite well for such a situation. It was simple enough to just have Alan (my butler) bring the it over (by the way, I have a bear rug in the study's as well, but that rug is polar bear, and I just really didn't think it would be smart to be getting sweaty and such on that. Dirt just shows up so easily on it, so there's no way I wanted to be jumping around on it in my loafers and smoking jacket! Funny thing about the polar bear rug, I actually got it from an auction of what was supposedly the late Elton John or some famous singer's estate back in 1987 I believe. It was crazy to get it from him and it's really such a tragedy he passed when he did. He made such good music too!! Just so terrible! Sometimes when I lie down on it I feel like I can almost hear some of his music playing. But, you know, as they say, the ladies do seem to love it though! And I'm not one to let a good bear skin go to waste!) so I could keep focused on the workout. I really hate to lose focus on non-essential things, and I didn't know what this tape would try to throw at me next!

The next exercise started and it was what referred to as "Warm Up." Here, overall, I think I did a bit better.

I had Alan come back over and assist me with what the video said was "stretching out those nasty, tight muscles," and I would say I even managed to actually get into things a little bit!

Surprisingly to my surprise it felt pretty good!

Pretty quick though, things went back to being confusing and bit off.

The next set of exercises involved mostly jumping around, dancing, and "moving and grooving those hips," as the video put it, to the sounds of 60's music.

I realized pretty quick that I was in over my head.

How was I expected to just gyrate around like that without hurting myself or just my general sense of pride or something?

No amount of warm up could prepare somebody for that kind of workout!

The additional people in the video must have all been actors or something to be able to pretend those things were so normal while such craziness was underway.

So, basically, due to this and because of it, I was left with no alternative but to have Alan take over for me with the workout tape. Meanwhile, as I was interested to see how things turned out for all those involved, I watched on while enjoying a bowl of pecan praline ice cream and a nice cigar.

It occurred to me during my second bowl of pecan praline what the true nature of the world of working out must be.

If this workout here was the best that could be offered even by the "king" of exercising, then how far off track must all the other workouts be?

No directions were provided beforehand, I did not feel any sense of actually working out my body, plus no person with even a small amount of self-esteem would be caught dead doing the workout.

I still really question whether to purpose of the videos was to get a workout or to just somehow take advantage of and make fun of those engaged in it like I ended up doing with Alan.

So, with this experience, I hope you can see just how able I am to criticize and question the idea of waking up in the morning and doing a bunch of "healthy" stuff to make yourself healthy.

I'm more than healthy enough, and I hardly ever even wake up to do anything!

FINAL THOUGHTS:

Remeber that guy Steve?

Well think about this: Steve most likely gets up in the morning and after getting ready, has an amazing "healthy" breakfast.

Afterward, he goes to the gym and works out for an hour and a half each morning to beat up his body and keep himself in good shape.

The silly people out there probably applaud Steve and think he is great and he's some sort of "winner" because he wastes his time everyday at the gym and getting all sweaty.

That's all a bunch of crap though!

Let's remember to not give into "the standard think."

There is no reason, not now, not ever, that you would ever need to start your day like that.

Who needs breakfast when there's always food at no matter what hour you get up?

Eat after you've had enough rest and your body get's itself up.

As I stated above, you can always sleep in this way and hit happy hour a bit early. We also learned that all business owners make great deals when their drunk.

So case closed. Battle won. Victory us. We did good boys, send 'em home.

You decide: do you want to not be a winner but a loser like Steve is? Or do you want to get up later when your good and ready to, hit the bar, and be you're on your way with a great, fun start to your day?

Oh and by the way., I know at this point you probably don't understand the "key" to this book. If you don't, you will.

Also, just a reminder, try not to listen to other people's advice unless it comes from me. Things will be much better for you that way.

CONCLUSION:

Well, I have to say, this is like pulling teeth. Writing out your thoughts in the "editor approved" way isn't easy, but he said I should have a conclusion to my thoughts, so here it is!

Why be an over-achiever when you can be a winner and take all the short-cuts and have all the fun that you want to have?

Stop before you start! You'll never fail to win if you never try to win!

So, I feel like I've given the loser Steve way too much credit and time in this section. We don't need to talk about him anymore. However, if you want to write in the blank areas of the page a few things that you think make him a loser, feel free.

I know I will!

P.S., A final point that I will mention is that I'm not saying I wake up regretting anything from prior days. I mean my life is awesome and we all tend to wake up remembering our prior days' wrongs and issues. Drinking can help is all I'm saying. Definitely lots of drinking to help with any issues that aren't but could be there.

Until next time,
Cheers!!

- Wally

Don't Eat Breakfast! Breakfast is for Losers! Steve is a Loser!

Editor's Note: *Know which rules you're breaking and why you're breaking them. There is nothing wrong with attempting to think creatively when you come up with a way to structure the content, but remember, the point of a book is to convey our ideas in a way the reader can follow.*

Any statistics you cite need to have proper references; unless you just made them up off the top of your head. You wouldn't do that though… right?

A meal can not be arrogant. It has no emotions and doesn't work on any level to add personification to it.

Should we really be encouraging people to go to bars in order to remove their feelings of unhappiness from prior days?

For the "workout" story, there are a number of problems here. First, you are admitting here to stealing a series of VHS tapes from a discount store? Additionally, I hardly feel that your negative experiences are indicative of the workout industry as a whole. You sounded underprepared and like you had somewhat misunderstood the intent of the workout tapes to begin with. Those tapes are designed for a much different audience. For example, my 50-something-year-old mother has had great success with the Richard Simmons workout series!

I feel that it's a given that most people, including business owners, do not make good decisions while they are drunk. We shouldn't be encouraging them to attempt to do so. What exactly are you basing that idea on, and what happens if they actually do this? You're just asking for a lawsuit!

Are you that upset that my "editor approved way" is trying to work on improving the structure and readability of this book?

The final "P.S." actually leaves me a bit concerned. Beyond seeing if you need help, I also don't think that's a great last thought to leave people with in this chapter.

Author's Response: I make great decisions while I'm

drunk! I'm drunk right now!

Dear Reader,

As you are now moving into what I would consider the body or "depths" of this book (although shallow), and in case you have still not taken an opportunity to make it through the Editor's Preface, I wanted to make one final appeal and heavily encourage you to please do so before continuing any further in this book.

I would also, again, like to strongly reiterate that this text was formatted without the complete agreement, planning, or proofing from myself, the book's editor, or the publisher.

As you move forward into the forthcoming pages, please understand that I only managed to work somewhat with the Joel/Wally on an edit of the first draft of this book, and specifically the first chapter. Due to frustrations felt by Joel/Wally, and some ongoing harassment directed towards me during the process, that is more or less as far as I was able to coach him directly.

All of this now being said, please proceed at your own risk and discretion! Thank you!

Get ready for the good stuff! - Wally

Chapter 2

Thoughts for this Chapter

You have no idea how difficult it is to condense my thoughts down into easy to understand, beautiful sentences!! Well structured phrasegology, and all the complex English writing things I know of and have done in order to help my writing to present my thoughts in the way they deserve and are clear.

As you've seen clearly in the first chapter, I know all about how to write about success and self-help in the standard formatted, lame-dame, self-help guide way of doing things.

I now want to do things my way!!

For this chapter, I combined my thoughts, expertise, and my actual and first and only hands experience with my style to provide this content for you.

Some thoughts may seem odd or perhaps even foreign to you, but I believe that you're smart and will get it when you really read it through.

You're not like Steve who I don't think he ever will.

Take your time, take notes, re-read, draw diagrams, build graphs and/or epitaphs and compare with others if you like!

This could be a great way to connect with other people marching down the path to find the keys to success themselves!

Editor's Note: *Why, specifically, do you feel it would be good for people to make epitaphs? What exactly are you expecting this book to do to readers?? Or is that something that just sounded like it fit so you included it?*

1

No matter how you slice it, people are for the most part selfish creatures and can't be trusted.

If you get nothing else from this self-help guide, I seriously hope you learn that it's hard to rely on people for nearly anythin! Anythin at all!

For some reason, people are unable to act without attempting to fulfill some personal want or desire within himself or theirself.

If you were to ask me to prove this, then I would probably say to you, "No! You prove it!"

But if I was then to decide to go ahead and do so out of my own desire and not because you asked me to, I would go about it this way--I'd like you to think about the fact that anything you have ever done in your entire life was only done because you wanted to get something from doing it.

Ponder that one nice, long, and hard!

For example, you buy a new car. Maybe you buy it because it helps you get around, maybe because you want something you can rely on and it gets good gas mileage, but your not gonna sit there and tell me you didn't also buy it because it makes you look like the s--- and awesome!

You think charity ain't selfish either? Everythin has a selfish personally beneficial aspect to it!

We like to hold up people who give donationable charitable donations as some sort of model of charity and selflessness, but isn't it also true that when people give they often talk about those wonderful nice fuzzies they get after they give?

Take a look at a few quotes from some "the standard think" type people below. And yes, as you would expect, I have written these out maybe not word-for-word, but in the heart and spirit of what they meant to mean:

"If you light a lamp for someone else, it will also be less dark around you because you just lit a lamp."
- Boodduh

"Happiness springs from doing good and helping others. And by 'helping others,' I mainly mean offering to buy a drink for them at the bar when they forgot their wallet."
- Playdo

"Give, and it will be given to you. A good measure, pressed down, shaken together and turn it all around. That is what it is all about."
- Jesus

"The best way to find yourself is to lose yourself in the moment of service of others. You only got one shot. One opportunity. Mom's spaghetti."
- Mahama Gandee

Do you see what the problem is now with these famous quotes??

Each and every single one of these people is so completely selfish!

Every thing they say is just about, do this thing so you can get more or be better, feel better, blah blah blah.

It's for this reason (that people are all selfish and for the most part just do what is best for them) that I ultimately say to myself, "I can do it better without um!"

Time for some personal application onto you.

Now that I have pointed all this out you can hopefully see that anyone who ever does anything for you in your entire life at any time really most likely did it because they had some selfish reason for it. They might likely have even only done it because they wanted to get something from you!

So, what is my goal for this section?

Well, in keeping with breaking from "the standard think" my goal for you in this section is to somehow help you to remove yourself from this messed up selfish system and call a spade a tool. Or a selfish person, if you will.

Why accept the fake generosity of some backhander giver, when you can learn to rely on yourself?

Better a sandwich from your butler than a steak dinner made by someone who just wants to get something from you, which is most likely money!

Maybe you're still stuck in "the standard think" thinking, and thinking, "This can't be true! There must be at least some way a person can act completely selflessly!"

Let me boggle and bewilder your mind.

Probably the only true way to do something with no selfish motive is to do something good out of hatred.

I mean, how could you be doing something selfish if you truly hate something but you help to improve it? That only works though if you are aren't doing something positive for something you hate in order to be able to let others know you were able to do it though, cause then you are still being selfish since it makes other people look at you better. So you either have to do something that you and everyone you know will hate, or you have to do whatever it is that you are doing in a way that not even you know you did it, like maybe with hypnotism or something? Or maybe black out drinking? Or maybe those under the influence of some kind of hallucinogenic drugs are the only ones who can be truly selfless??

With all this said, I absolutely still don't think there is any way of doing much of anything without at least some motive of selfish gain.

The big difference for me though, and where I'd like you to eventually get to, is that I don't deny the selfish nature in myself or others. Instead, I work it, flip that thing down and reverse it, and sometimes even encourage myself in it.

Once you can come to the realization that being selfish is

inevetiable, there's almost no alternative!

With this bit of knowledge, you will no longer be stuck within a negative pattern of "the standard think," trying to balance your selfish actions with self-less actions. Since all actions are selfish, you can just act selfishly all you want!

Most of the people in the world walk around on complete auto-self-pilot.

Like Steve, they engage in the same thought patterns and ways of action out of a simple desire to not upset what they have learned to do and to keep life simple.

This being the case, and with the understanding that people are unstoppably, unbendingly selfish, people will always default into a selfish mode of operation.

With this positive note covered (that all people are selfish, including you, and will never have a way of breaking free from it), let us now move on to the main point of this chapter.

Editor's Note: *This is an overall note for this section of chapter 2. While I can understand your feeling that people act in a selfish manner quite often (something I currently understand quite well), do you really believe humanity can only be selfish? That somehow putting someone else's needs above your own can be considered selfish just because it results in you feeling good? If anything, I think it would be better to measure everything on a scale of how much or little of their actions are selfishly motivated, and not just treat it in an all or nothing fashion. Human emotions and motivations are complex ideas. Either way, I'm really not sure that the result of just not trusting anyone is realistic or healthy. I feel it would still be better to push people towards caring for and about others despite the selfishness we all experience at times.*

You have gotten all of the quotes spot on, really, just tremendous job there. You may just want to do a quick search to confirm you didn't potentially replace a few words or misspell a few names.

If you're planning to "boggle and bewilder" someone's mind, do you realize that means you are surprisingly confusing them?

I'm not sure it's a good idea to really suggest our readers should do things out of hatred. That seems like it is the precursor to major acts of crime and attacks on others after reading this book. Either way, you seem to have gotten pretty significantly lost in the point here and can cut out almost all of the paragraph on finding out how to commit truly "selfless" acts.

Author's response: You're so stuck in thinking you're own dumb thinking you don't even know it!! I know how to handle my hatreds very well, thank you! If I didn't, I wouldn't even be talking to you! Oh, and I imagine my readers will understand well too when they read what I'm saying!

2

The main point in understanding this concept is not to just harp on the selfish stuff and attitudes, but it's so you can understand that you are really the only person you can ever really trust. And for the better or the worse, this is not to say that you can ever really 100% trust yourself either!

I mean, how many times have you told yourself, "Hey, no more hunting expeditions this year. Six is plenty!" Only to find yourself calling Alan and telling him to book you another week long at the The Point so you can head back out to the forest for some good old fashioned bear tracking?

People engage in activities all the time they have no desire to, but can't keep themselves from doing. You end up doing something you've told yourself over and over and over and over again that you will never ever do that thing over and again.

We, as a human, we will also trick myself into thinking that you are sometimes doing something because it is the right thing or it is the good thing despite knowing that it will most likely end in your own pain and suffering.

If you are going to put yourself in harm's way on purpose, then you truly can't trust yourself even all that much to do what's best for yourself.

So, what can you do?

It's like a rock and a stuck place!

Given the alternative, trusting other people who have nothing but selfish motives and are also engaging in self-destructive activities, trusting yourself is still probably your best option. Us as individuals are still the trustworthiest to ourselves out of the bunch. We are our own best enemy and friend.

You might be wondering at this point, "What h--- does this have to do with success?"

If so, then calm down some please and let me tell you!

If you want to become successful and break away from that dumb "the standard think," you have to understand the selfish and untrustworthy nature of the world around you, and then figure out how to deal! With it!

How many of you are at all familiar with the Pareto Principle?

Some of you may be. Me being as well educated on matters such as success and business and philosophizing as myself am, I am very familiar and will now explain it!

People like to think that the optimal way and standard way that things break down is into nice little 50% packages. Half the time is this, half the time it's that, optimally. The Pareto Principle was proposed by an Italian bloke at some point and flips the whole flipper on its head. Basically, he figured out that things rarely ever break down into a true 50/50 split, but will more often break down into categories of 80/20.

Examples would be something like:

20% of your work accounts for 80% of profits.

Or,

20% of your drinking accounts for 80% of your drunkenness.

This principle is something that I would highly encourage you to work into your thinking on how you interact with others and whill be pursuing success.

Basically, how this plays out for me and should for you is that you trust everyone else about 20% and put trust in yourself at about 80%.

You try to live by 80%-20% when it comes to the amount that you will receive from others too.

With this, the impact that others can make on you through any self-centered ways can be kept to a totally significant minimum and you'll be able to just let your own selfish tendencies mostly be your guide!

Editor's Note: *So, your concept is that people can't trust others, and people can't trust themselves, so how would someone keep from becoming a completely untrusting and paranoid person this way? Beyond being completely obtuse and unaware of reality? Ah...*

And some people actually consider it a skill and a part of healthy character to be able to do the things that they need to despite it potentially causing some pain or suffering. It's a concept of short-term versus long-term gain.

Also, the person behind the "Pareto principle" is Vilfredo Pareto. It is primarily supposed to be applied as a principle behind inputs and outputs in sales & business. Not as a measure of relationships, and especially not as a measure of how someone should be drinking!

Author's response: Conceptually, what's with the "ah..."?? Did you figure something out?

Editor's Note: *Yes, you could say that.*

3

One final item before finishing this side of self-help will a full helping of successfulness!

I'd like to mention a bit the best approaches to take with sharing in someone's abilities, talents, and very importantly, their knowledge and information.

Sometimes, and although I will generally advise against working with others, it becomes necessary to rely on the talents and services of others around you.

If you're working a business deal, or some sort of negotiation, or sometimes work just needs to get done that you really don't want to do yourself cause it's boring or dumb, well at those times the assistance that another person can offer you will be just the right amount of leverage to help you get what you want.

Thanksfully, when treated with the right amount of caution and attention, working with someone else can be navigated in at least a somewhat less frisky fashion.

The biggest "key" to this is to always make sure that you are the primary person who will gain from whatever is that you are working together to achieve. When you stand to gain the most, the risk is sometimes better to put yourself through!

Also, perhaps you are wise and you are already doing this (and if not, begin as soon as you absolutely can), but when it comes to what you can give to the person you are working with to help you find success, do your absolutely best to suppress, withhold and keep to yourself all knowledge, time, abilities, money, and anything you can. This goes for everyone. Clients, partners, employees, helpers, pets, volunteers, or pretty much anyone else.

Remember, they're selfish too, so they don't deserve anything from you: time, money or otherwise!

Plus, the withholding of crucial information can often be a lifesaver if s--- hits the s--- fan and help prevent you from facing off against disloyalty amongst the rank and file.

If you hand over too much info, you might find that those people could eventually work themselves into having a stronger and stronger grip on your success when it finally does arrive.

Or, like Steve, they could even try to stop you from it just to be a jerkwad who doesn't know anything!!

One principle I live the life I live by is that I never pay for time and services from others that I can get for free from somewhere else. Give it enough time and Alan will usually be able to find some free labor somewhere, even if it's just on through Craigslist or something.

If they provide decent work and demand payment, then they easiest way to find this is to just help them understand they are providing a service to something amazing (your tremendous success), so that alone should be enough to motivate them to help you.

The fact they they will be able to list this help they are providing on their personal resumes after you're awesomely successful like me should completely be gift enough for them!

If you must offer some type of payment, perhaps do something very simple and treat them to a meal or coffee. Coffee is simple to make (I've never actually made coffee for myself, but it seems like a process that would be simple but gross. It's a liquid that comes from a bean which, I mean, that just seems weird to me), cheap, and makes people feel like they really are absolutely and completely appreciated even when that's totally not the case.

Just watch how people react when you offer to buy them coffee or food when they are volunteering work for you. They act like it is the greatest gift known to personkind! It's almost dumb how dumb that is.

And if you're like me and can't stand being around them, do like I do and just have someone every once in awhile call and tell them off them until you get what you want from them!

Never ever forget, that unless someone is willing to pay you significant money for an opportunity for you to be hired by them, and they are giving you a big fat retainer, and you are actually will be the one calling the shots, then you should probably just turn them down.

You never ever want to accidently find yourself caught with your pants down and someone else is calling the shots.

Editor's Note: *Should we really be encouraging individuals to use other people just to get what they want and when they stand to gain the most? Wouldn't it be more worthwhile to make things mutually beneficial if possible? Why does working towards success mean you have to be self-centered in this way?*

What does being selfish with a pet accomplish? And now you're just coaching people to be selfish since others are selfish? This sounds like a lesson you should have learned in school as a child, but isn't it sometimes better to give than receive? Won't that make life much better for all?

Additionally, wouldn't you agree that if you can help others find success then that can end up helping you just as much?

It's amazing to me how much your taking advantage of others is now actually starting to sound like theft from them or at least a type of fraud. Most people would not argue that you shouldn't try to trick people into work and then just offer them a coffee or a meal since that will make them happy enough. A worker is worth their wages!

Lastly, your comment on having someone call to harass a person you are working with makes a lot of sense to me... for some reason.

Author's Response: Did someone call you and spoil your poor little day?? Hahahahahahaah!!

Chapter 3:

"The Standard Think" Breaker
Success Assignment

Read Virgil's "Georgics" book III, then head to the next chapter!

Editor's Note: *This does not call for its own chapter. You can certainly encourage readers to study outside works for additional points you are wanting to make, but you've provided no description of the purpose people should get from reading this.*

Additionally, it's quite the random reference that appears to have no connotations to any "self-help" style points or concepts! Did you just randomly search for books and this popped up?

Author's Response: You gotta break free before you can break in! "The standard think" demands it!

Editor's Note: *I both would and wouldn't like to know what exactly it is you are trying to break into.*

Play by your own rules

Call back Tiffany!! -xoxo

Arctic Ocean translates to
Bear Ocean! Whaaaa?!

You Mr. sir, are a very
important person who
people think is awesome, so
go be awesome!

Educate, education, and
all that learning stuff -to
do!

Dry cleaning? Find out
what it is. #Hint: Alan makes
trips there!!

DO IT! DO IT! DON'T NO
DO IT!!

...life with just do whatever we want to do??

...the ocean with a heli-pad... and juices. You can buy yourself... according... around a busted up car instead of... have Alan clean it up, or drive the car, or burn... like Steve, but of course a choice idiot like him... the point is, money will set you free! You will have freed... into thinking that... choice.

Even if a few want to come up together... you are still having freedom... which means you think... able to be progressing... which means you are also close to being successful or at least in your... somehow, listening to this type of dumb thinking... then lead to you... stupid filthy rich.

Think about this for a second, someone like Steve may not

Subject: "Info" on Steve

Arnie <arnold.waxter@waxterlaw.com>

Thu, Feb 2, 2017 at 3:56 PM

To: Wally <wallstotheballs5@gmail.com>

Hi Wally!

Attached below is the information I was able to track down through my connections for the guy you wanted to know about. I know you mentioned wanting to get as much dirt as possible, but it unfortunately appears to be a situation where there isn't really much in the way of dirt.

A few highlights:

- Born in Baltimore, MD in 1981.
- Attended the prestigious McDonogh School.
- Took numerous extracurriculars and AP courses while attending there.

- Received athletic and education scholarships to attend Duke in 1999. Graduated top of his class/with honors in 2003, then went on to get his Master's degree at Johns Hopkins University.
- High School and collegiate athlete with several fitness awards. Tried out for Olympics but just missed the mark. Won numerous education awards.

There is a lot more listed in the attached doc, so check that out as you like.

I hope the info helps in some way.

Lastly, please please please, Wally, give me a call soon to discuss the WOBI event! The event managers have been hitting me up pretty heavy about the event debacle and the costs of repairs! We really need to respond with something!!!

<Steve_notes.docx>

Arnold Waxter, Esq.
The Waxter Lawfirm

want to choose a "rich" lifestyle, but the level of influence that the rich have is almost unreal.

You can make your own lofty dreams come true as well as those around you, so why wouldn't it come with influence?

How do you think I got this book published even??

I think we'll talk about this later, but even though I am well known as being such an amazing successful person and educator (or "the king of success" as some should call me) who absolutley should be writing about success, it's still really hard to get a book published.

If I didn't have all this super tasty cash on hand to invest in the process, it probably would have taken a lot longer to get published!

And again, a lot of this is because, like Alan, with cash, you can surround yourself with people to do all your bidding.

Got a messy task that needs cleaning up? Well, lets just get "the boys" to take care of that. I mean, wouldn't you rather be the one sending out "the boys" to do something for once instead of you always being sent as one of "the boys"?

Do you ever wonder why they say, "It takes money to make money"? Well they say that because it is very true! When you have all the money, then you can use that money to build a money fortress that nobody can get into. I mean, not like a literal one, although, I mean, you could probably make a literal fortress made of money if you have enough of it but people could probably just burn it down or use a big fan, I don't know. No, what I mean is that with cash you can pretty easily set rules to favor you to keep you finding success.

Think about it: You could grease some palms, you could stack a jury, you could potentially even get some laws changed or added if need be to help out a few of your more lucrative investments if they're important enough to you and you could stand to gain a lot.

A final pictoral metaphor to end this section with -- assume that success is like a smelly, overweight and hairy man attempting to court and swoon a beautiful woman.

This beautiful women will run from him in a second; scared of the mere look and smell of him and the thought of just having to spend time around him.

But with the right kind of money, things might just go differently for the super ugly smelly man! He can afford to pay someone to help him get less smelly, hairy, and overweight and the girl might end up being interested because he also has a ton of money!!

Truly, the at the heart of success is a giant wad of cash.

Editor's Note: *Money is now more important than purpose or meaning?*

I find your significantly oversized list of the different naming iterations for money impressive, but also quite revealing and troubling. How can you knowingly list all these terms so effortlessly yet misunderstand the structure of a simple sentence?

We should not ever encourage our readers to purchase people! This is a joke, correct?

Also, I have to ask, do you truly believe that money will give you happiness? Has that truthfully been your experience, or are you just saying that because it's what you've heard or are used to thinking? Plus, wouldn't doing something to help others or at least using your money for a good cause bring more to people?

Does adding the word "designer" just make items sound more expensive and luxurious to you?

What pop-culture zombie movie did you base your idea on that a zombie invasion is soon to be coming? Do you really want to waste your words and our reader's time, attention, and efforts that could be spent working towards success, attempting to "help" them prep for the ridiculously ludicrous idea of a coming zombie invasion?

I'm amazed at how you've managed to bring around the idea of pursuing success, to pursuing money, to pursuing freedom, to being

American, and all the way back to pursuing success. It's quite a crazy path.

Lastly, the story of the ugly man and the girl ended much better than I had assumed it would. Good job on that.

Author's response: You joke about the zombies, but it's a thing man! And when it happens, guess who's not getting invited into my super-secret underground end-of-the-world designer bunker? That's right! Mmhmm!

2

Many, many other stupid self-help books that you might read will teach you that success comes through other means besides money.

Maybe they feel like it's good or something to manage it, but a lot of times they ignorantely teach that it'll take a ton of time and work and effort to become successful as well.

In truth, it can absolutely take a bunch of amount of time to become successful and make a bunch of money money moolah, but I have also known many successful people for that which it can happen in a very short amount of time!

Going from shopping at discount stores to buying all your stuff at designer supermarkets, a true indication of success, can sometimes be an instant thing for people who are lucky enough to stumble upon a metaphorically lucky golden lotto ticket.

This could be an actual honest-to-goodwin winning lotto ticket, or maybe they get in early on the ground level of the hotest new pyramid scheme. Or perhaps, and this is probably the best way I know, perhaps they figure out some fancy way of setting up some ongoing source of money from someone to keep something (documents, photos, videos, or the "big three" of the extortion world I call them) from getting out that could affect the first person in some really awfully bad way!

Whatever way you look at it, people seem to put an unreasonable amount of importance on the concept of time and its worth.

People even like to say time has value, but do you think that this is actually true?

In my non-"the standard think" thinking, time pretty much has no value at all. Not only that, if it does somehow magically have some value, it really doesn't add up to much!

The grandiosiest reason for this it the obvious truth that we all have exactly as much time as the next person.

Everybody has exactly as much time as their life lasts and then they die and then they don't have any more time. You're gonna die! I'm gonna die! But are you gonna really live!?

Because of all this, to summarize, I don't think there really exists a way of assigning value for time.

For some, they might have a ton of time left, but for others, maybe only a little. One of us could and likely is dropping dead as a doorknob as they read this right now!

Freaky!!

That's pretty disgusting actually!

Anyway, you should assume that since we have no idea how much time is left before the sun explodes, or there's a massive meteor smashing into us, or some zombie-end-of-the-world catistrophicapalness such and such happens, that it's best to try your best to not even think about it.

In addition, the worth of time I can tell you is both irrelativant as well as relativant.

For example, below I've listed a few different kinds of people that actually exist within the world. I would like for you to take a moment to break away from "the standard think" and ponder about them and what relativant or irrelaivant value time has for each of them:

- A wealthy aristocratic oil baron has so much money that it can afford to occupy other people's time in addition to their own. They spend their days yachting, smelling lovely things, fencing, traveling to fancy places like Denver, hunting, dancing and dining all while other people do whatever they want.

- A guy is in the hospital in a vegetable state due to an on-the-job accident and will remain in that state for the remainder of his boring, lazy years. Since he can't do anything but lay around, he has nothing but time on his hands.

- An OCD mental patient who spends every waking moment obsessed with simple not important tasks like washing their hands, counting peas and toothpicks over and over, not stepping on cracks, and numerous other obsessions. They have no time to be doing anything besides obsess about their OCDs.

Do you see now with these amazing explanations I have provided to you how time can be very much different for every person?

One person can have tons of time to do whatever, but another has basically a non-stop schedule of things to be do. Or for one person time doesn't matter since they can do whatever they want, while for another person they just want time to stop. The possible time examples are nearly endless.

Like for me, I place very little value in time most of the time, but then at other times I place a whole ton of value in time. For example, when I have a speaking engagement, I could pretty much care less about how much time or anything they have me scheduled for since I probably won't show up anyway. But when I order Alan to make me a meal, I care very much about time since I'll have to be sitting there waiting and eagerly anticipating eating it until he finally gets done making it!

A good example of a time waster for me where time literally was wasted that I wish I could get back was when I went to see a movie a little while back. Based upon what I was thinking, the movie would be this super funny story about some super-rich millionaire parents dying in a skiing accident or something and leaving their infant baby with this big old massive fortune that they would then spend in ridiculous fashion. What would a baby spend all those millions on? Funny hijinks, hilarity, and craziness ensues. But noooo, the movie was just about this dumb girl with father issues setting up some elaboratly cumbersome plot to commit suicide. What does that even have to do with anything? Time wasted!

Beyond all this and to add more to the point, it's not like you can purchase more time from like the "time store" down the block, so it would be really inaccurate to say that time has much of any worth in money.

Time exists outside of our ability to turn into a pill or some kind of goo or paste, then bottle up, and so we can't buy it, sell it, or alter it in any way.

Like some character from a storybook, time will wait for nobody, and will continue moving on in whatever way it wants, quite stubbornly, although that direction will probably forward. I'm not some time scientist who knows about such things in specific, but I'm just saying I've never heard or scene time moving any other direction outside of a superhero movie or something!

So if I can wrap this up nicely with a bow, what this "key" boils down to in regards to time and success, if you're really paying attention and working to break free of that "the standard think," is that since time is uncontrollable and really shouldn't be seen as having any actual value, procrastination and deferring action can be a "key."

Procrastination can be the "key" to moving from simply just getting something done to getting the right things done in the right way at the right time.

Think about it, if you were honest with yourself, don't both you and I both procrastinate the things that we don't want to do?

Why is that?

Well I'll tell you why because there is a d--- good reason for it!

Procrastination is a sign of knowing what it is that your body wants and allowing it to influence your actions.

Sometimes your body will want to move quickly with something and get it done, and you should do that. "Let your body do the talking for your mind and body," as they say.

If you want to quickly take action to get something done and taken care of then do it and don't stop even if you face difficulties, or critics, the authorities, dementia, or even "haters" telling you how horrible a job you are doing or that you are wrong in some way and might get into significant farscicle "felonious" trouble! They most likely don't have even any warrant on you to stop you from doing what you're doing.

Just tell them you are doing what your body wants you to do. Then you can figure out what went wrong once you're done!

That's pretty much all I ever say, and it seems to work for me pretty much most of the time. So, that should be all the explanation you need.

Other times, your body might desire a more lakadakadaisicle approach, and you should choose to embrace your body at that time as well.

Basically, you shouldn't look at procrastination as a sign of weakness.

Instead, you should consider the procrastinating you do as just your body asking you to give it the time it needs to prepare and adjust as it should. It will often prevent you from injuring yourself, both emotionally, physically, or spiritually, from not being prepared.

Like an athlete that needs to stretch, and exercise, and prepare before competing on the field of battle, you might need to prep yourself!

And don't be concerned too much if it takes a long time for you to break free of your procrastination.

It might take days, months, or even years for you to get around to completing something you have a responsibility for, but please please please just go right ahead and let people know that although you might understand their concern for your procrastinatiousness, your body just isn't ready yet.

Overall, the natural cycle your body is gonna take with processes and tasks is something you should never force to be something other than what it is; otherwise, you can truly end up hurting yourself and preventing any success in the future.

If you end up pushing your body too fast or too slow, you could end up seriously hampering your ability to do the work in the right way at the right time, and you don't want that!

Not unless you are living off of disability*, in which case you might just want to go the other directions with things.

Lastly, just by reading this book, I guarantee you that you are gonna be leaps and bountifuls beyond where most people are on their path to finding success and breaking free of "the standard think," so you deserve a bit of time to let your body just enjoy itself and where it's at.

*If you're a reader living off disability, could you please get in contact with me at some point? Nothing crazy or strange at all. Just have a few questions for a close friend of mine about how that works and how you got on with getting on it. He or she friend of mine might actually be trying to get on it at some point too for completely legitimate medical issues they are having or have had as well from what I've heard.

Editor's Note: *Did you realize it sounds like you are calling your book stupid in your first paragraph?*

You are likely setting yourself up for some major issues to hint that pyramid schemes and extortion could be good ways of making money!

I'm not sure if you realized how this all added up in your description, but when encouraging the readers to find success and working towards it, it may not be the best idea to remind them that time doesn't have worth, they're eventually gonna die, and that the people reading the book are possibly dying. That realistically won't instill a strong sense of confidence in your book, but additionally in working toward success or much of anything, for that matter, if they were to take it to heart!

I think you are confusing the idea that time has a value due to the fact that you only have a limited amount of it with the idea that people are actually thinking you can sell time. Saying that time has "value" means that it is limited and shouldn't be taken advantage or wasted.

Perhaps you should go into a movie considering more than just the title as the sole indicator for what the film might contain. I think the trailer and marketing alone made it pretty apparent you were in for a much different film than what you were expecting.

People can often times procrastinate things they want and need to do just as easily as the things they don't want to do. Beyond your personal opinion, what study or example could you actually point to that shows procrastination is a good measure of what is or isn't what someone should be doing? You should be blaming laziness or work ethic more so than making excuses for procrastination.

You absolutely should consider stopping if the "authorities" are telling you to! Warrant or no warrant, you absolutely should!

While I agree that it's good not to push one's self so far and so fast that one ends up getting hurt, shouldn't more time be spent encouraging people to at least push themselves and stretch themselves to grow? Is it really that wrong for us to think that through pushing ourselves we are able grow in our abilities, character, and can be more effective in life, among many many other good reasons?

Author's response: Nobody said nothing about that people should actually extort others, I'm just saying it can work!

3

It's tedious and tiring. It's hard and frequently pops up when you'd least like for it to. And worst of all, it's almost always related to something you don't want it to be about!

You know what it is!! Let's say it alllll togetherrrr!! Haaaard work!

"Hard work," as I call it, fails to do anything more for than just keep you busy with dumb stuff that "needs to be completed." Which is exactly how I define it. Hard things to do that need to be done.

And if there is one thing I've learned over the course of my couple years on this earth and all the experiences I've gotten to go through and experienced, it's that hard work is only ever done by people who aren't capable of getting other people to do it for them.

More than just having other people do any random thing for you, I am talking about giving work to other people that you specificelly don't want to do. Specificelly, this is what is otherwise known as "denigration," or "delegation." Which delegation sounds better to many I think, so we'll stick with that.

Delegation is not only something that you need to learn at some point, but also an art form for be mastered. "The Art of Delegations" (***GREAT IDEA! REMINDER TO TALK TO ARNIE ABOUT WHAT "™"s ARE AND GETTING ONE***) comes down to how you can weave a task around someone that allows you to take control over them and so then get them to take care of the hard work that would otherwise fall on you.

Each person you are delegating to can be a line or verse. cog and a cog winder. dog and a fire hydrant? (***ADD SOMETHING POETIC SOUNDING OR SONG-LIkE AND DEEP***) that all comes together to form one beautiful ball of freedom from undesirable tasks.

Someone who is successful and has learned "The Art of

Delegations" can accomplish the most incredible feats of pawning of things they don't want to do. They can have even random people doing everything from picking up their dog from the doggy day-care, to reading bedtime stories to their kids at night, to taking their elderly, fragile aunt with dementia for walks down at the care center.

So for those of you who are reading this and really serious about working towards success, I would start implementing this "key" of "The Art of Delegations" as soon as you are able!

A great place to start is by actually letting others around you know that you are trying to learn how to delegate. From there, most people should agree to letting you tell them what to do in order to learn this skillful artform.

And if not, you can always do what I do and just start delegating until they listen.

Just so you aren't completely entering this tossed salad, the "key" to this whole delegation thing is to really work to find what type of "Delegation Approach" (***"TM" FOR THIS AS WELL!!***) works best for you when delegating. Due to your "the standard think" (***ACTUALLY, MAYBE A "TM" FOR THIS ONE TOO? IS THERE A LIMIT??***) you may be wondering what exactly I mean by the idea of your "Delegation Approach"TM"."

Well, by this term I am referring to the special way that you and only you (unless you're an identical twin) use different styles of approaching people in order to delegate things to them.

Since you aren't likely sure quite what I am saying exactly quite yet, I have worked and pondered and puzzled my brain to effectively write out what I personally (just by me, and nobody else helped me with these amazingly enough) consider some of the key approaches that exist and I myself have been known to use.

These are provided below for you to consider as you're just starting out here.

And do just that. Consider and ponder these not "the standard think" ideas of delegation appraoches and then take a few hours maybe to decide for yourself which one or all of them fit you best*:

The "Won't You Be My Neighbor?" Approach™:

Some call this humble, others compassionate, I just call it weak and loserly.

This approach involves somehow convincing those around you to take on tasks through being considerate and respectful, but to me, it is the generally least reliable or effective means to approach a person for delegation.

You're approaching people out of a sense of weakness, as if you think they will not want to help you or be willing to if you apply a bit more force. Like they might have something better they should be doing.

Consideration with people will only get you so far. Since people are so selfish, you are likely to get a ton of folks that just flat out say, "No way!" Those who agree will also just do so to try and be nice but you know their heart won't be truly in it!

The Bryan Mills Approach™ :

Basically you approach people in a very aggressive, unapologetic manner and treat what you are trying to get them to do as a command and not as a request.

I find that this approach works well if you can get people to listen, but it will often depend on the context of the situation for when it'll work. If it's people who are working for you already, it works pretty great! If it's anyone else, there's a really good chance they'll just not allow you to tell them what to do.

If you in have access to a few "strong arms" then this may be a very great option for you. That will help a ton and you might be able to make this forceful approach a bit more forceful.

P.S., In truth, I would just let you know that from my experiences, about half the time I use this approach people can definitely respond in a pretty negative way! Be prepared for potential shouting and fisticufs! Thankfully, I have Alan for just such an occasion to fake a heart condition when they don't respond as they should.

The Mr. Howell approach™ :
As we already discussed, money talks baby!! It says, "Hey! How would you like to do something for me and then you can go buy yourself some food, or a coffee, or those new hip and toasty sneakers you've been wanting for so long?"

If not for the fact that it's always better to spend money on you instead of giving it to others, this might actually be the best way of actually motivating those around you to do what you're asking from them. I mean, how do you think I can boss Alan around as much as I do? Of course, when you're as wealthy as I am it doesn't really matter if you have to pay money. I just really don't like doing it!

The "Wally" Approach™:
I have named this "approach" after me because although this form of delegation is probably the trickiest to master, it is for sure my absolute favorite and the best one if you can learn it!

I'm talking about delegation through manipulation and cunningness. Why is it so great?

Overall, manipulation makes delegation gets you what you want but and frees you from the need to pay people for their help! Which is beautiful! Also, there's very little danger of them getting violent with you (unless they randomly figure out what's happening which barely ever happens), and you don't have to worry so much about working with them on something.

How does it work?

Here's a few "keys" I've put together through the years on how to go about it that are actually differentions on the approach itself:

The "Wally" Approach v1:

Start off with a very unreasonable request (move this boulder, sell your house, go kill yourself) then follow it with a more reasonable one. If people think they're getting off light, they will be more likely to accept!

The "Wally" Approach v2:

Make your first request unusual then follow it up with a more normal one. They will be more likely to follow through on the second considering the first was just crazy!

For example, I once requested for my lawyer, Arnie "Arnold" Waxter, to find me a small, uninhabited and unclaimed island so that I could claim it as my own and establish it as a sovereign nation called Wallyfordania. I knew he'd flip out and all that (he's such a nervous fellow) and would say that he couldn't, so I just followed it up with a request to set up a bear hunting excursion service in Central Park, which is much more reasonable obviously.

The "Wally" Approach v3:

If you have the means, you can try to inspire fear in the hearts of those who you're wanting to manipulate, by threatening or the threat of threatening, then provide them relief from the threat. They'll be so releaved they are bound to help you!

The "Wally" Approach v4:
Make the person feel super and very absolutely amazingly guilty. Get them feeling that they are just worse than an algae covered monkfish and you'll have them eating out of your hand!

The "Wally" Approach v5:
And perhaps my favorite of all time, pertend like you are the victim of some horrible things who just needs help somehow! Don't want to pay for some ridiculous medical bill? Convince the billers you also need help because you had your identity stolen and all your money taken. Works for me all the time!

Ultimately, this approach is still as simple as deciding to tell someone what they need to hear instead of maybe what they want to hear. And I truly feel that in a sense, this approach can actually be the most fair and respectful way to delegate to others since they don't even know what hit them, plus prevent other's selfishness from hurting us.

We can't all be like Steve who faints at the simple thought of a mistruth being uttered in his presence!

So, with these approaches listed, again, take the time to study and understrand them. Then, when you feel comfortable enough with one or the whole lot of them, give them a test out on some random folks to see how they work for you!

You will soon start to see how your delegatin can give

you a God-blessedly fun means to remove hard work from your-self and move yourself into a state where you're able to 100% focus on simply your own "Path to Success ™"!

*Need not to worry now readers!

I realized as I was writing all this that I can't possibly extrapicate and dissegimate all of the awesome ideas to their fullest in this little section. Additionally, neither can I for all the bajillions of other great thoughts I have on life and success and breaking free of "the standard think" in this book alone.

Trust me, people couldn't handle too much of me at once considering how dense I can be with all of my writing!

So, to fix this obvious issue, I'm excited to announce that I plan to write a very much loved and highly anticipated follow up book about success and the key tennants of how to lead people in a really good way and such, so definitely be on the lookout for that! I have one other idea that seems to be making lots of money and helping writers find success too, so we'll see!

Editor's Note: *First, I will say that your introduction to the concept of "hard work" sounds vague, unrelated, and somewhat... suggestive.*

I think you included the word "couple" there when you should not have.

Mr. Malone might be interested to hear that you are attempting to trademark the term "The Art of Delegation."

What person would want to find just any random person to delegate things such as reading bedtime stories to their kids or helping their elderly aunt, too? These seems like quite dangerous and risky ideas to suggest!

Do you sincerely not understand the idea that "™" is an abbreviation of "trademark"?

There are numerous problems with aspects of all of the "delegation

*approaches" you have listed, but primarily, your final one entitled,
"'Wally' Approach v5" just exceedingly stands out as having issues.
I'm not sure where you are headed with this, but it sounds like you
are wanting people to study the art of becoming a con artist. If you
have to include it these ideas, can't you formulate this approach
more around the idea of using emotional appeals or something
along those lines, which would at least make it less apt to cause
lawbreaking?*

*On your note at the end of this section, how could people be "highly
annticipated [sic]" a follow-up book when you still haven't published
this one yet? Additionally, and I am not generally one to give up in
the face of extreme hardship (I believe our challenges can make
us stronger when faced correctly), but I am praying and strongly
encouraging you to ponder the arduous process we have already
gone through in creating this book and perhaps reconsider your
desire to publish a second. I'm truthfully concerned how much more
the general reading public might suffer were you to actually write
another self-help book such as you've indicated.*

Author's response: You're the sic one, man. Youre a sic
man!! And its "THE 'Wally' Approach v5," not "'Wally Approach," moron! We've used our words for reasons that are
important!

Editor's Note: *Agreed that we generally do use our words for important
reasons. With you, however, I have yet to see strong proof of this.*

4

In this section, I want to share with you an important story that plays into this whole concept of how to make and keep money. And it has to do with this: People want to tell you that there's no such thing as a free lunch, but I can tell you from personal experience that there actually is such thing as a "free lunch," you just need to know where to look!

And no, I'm not referring to dumpster diving or something like that.

I gonna share with you below this little story of mine to help explain exactly what it is I am talking about. While I am, be sure to take more notes and also make sure you aren't falling too far into the d--- "the standard think" like we talked about!

A little while back, as is normal for me, I was offered a tremendously lucrative speaking engagement by one of the usual prestigious and super popular conference groups that I am often invited to speek for.

Thanks to my work, and planning, and tremendous successes, and possibly because I've marketed myself this way, many consider me an amazing speaker for conferences like these all around the globe, and so my reputation precedes me on getting certain kinds of conference speaking bookings. And although I am not at liberty discuss or mention (Arnie advised me against doing so) who they are, I will let you know that many of the groups that I am retained by for speaking are some of the most powerful, secretive segments of some very lucrative industries. Trust me on this!

This speaking gig was no joke either. We're talking big bucks! Mucho Robert De Niro!

As is my standard operandie with these bookings, I quickly accepted the gig and had them transfer over the retainer fee to my account.

I then proceeded to my standard phase two of the process by feeding them an excuse for why I wouldn't be able to make it to the event.

Thanks to Alan and his cleverness (seriously, Alan really is so clever at times), I informed the conference organizers through Arnie that I would unfortunately be predisposed due to a last minute lupectomy.

Now of course I didn't *actually* have to get a lupectomy. I am not even sure what that is, but it's not like I am some sort of unhealthy beast! The main thing was that I had to have a good reason not to speak, and fortunately since I already had the money there shouldn't have been any problems. This should have been my "free lunch," but that would come later.

The unfortunate part of the story is that I didn't expect the conference group to be so litigious and persnickety. The conference folks started getting all fussy, since I guess I had apparently on some prior occasion already potentially backed out of a speaking engagement with them and had held onto the retainer for that, and something something about me not being actually sick.

So, after arguing it out and a bunch of back and forth with the the conference people through Arnie for a good long while, it basically came down to the fact that if I didn't end up going then they were very likely going to try and bring me up on charges of yada-yada-yada, and per Arnie, due to blah-blah-blah, someone might find out some additional information that they really didn't need to know about me and/or potentially expose me to certain investigations which would cause me a ton of issues... you've heard this stuff before I'm sure, so I'll just summarize to say that I didn't want to have them looking too deeply into my bits and pieces.

So, I was more or less on the hook for this one! Or I should more clearly say that so they thought that I thought that I was on the hook for this one!

But you know, there's more than one way to shave a porpoise as they say!

Sure they could force me to attend and speak, but thankfully, over years of practice and the entirely infrequent occasions where this has happened to me in the past, I have put together a plan which I feel more than works for this type of situation. It's a plan I call the "Malarkey Method."

I arrived the day of the scheduled conference with my "method" ready to go, and true to my speaking agreement, gave them a speech that was and is likely the best they are ever to have seen before or will ever to have seen!

I started things off with a peppering of motivational songs to get the crowd going and revved up. Nothing gets folks going like a 15-20 minute loop of "Thunderstuck" by AC/DC!!

Next, I mixed in a mashup of motivational video clips from famous films -- the coach giving a pep-talk during halftime while their team is down by 50, the mom telling her kid that he is the greatest and will one day achieve his dreams if he just keeps working hard, the man on the horse with magical sword in the air about to charge a battlefield full of orcs and giving his troops one last encouraging speech. All the quality, standard, realistic motivational scenes from famous films that people connect so well with.

Then, just when things were starting to really get going, I busted out the re-enactments of recordings of famous historical speeches. Jeff Daniels reading "The Gettysburg Address," "The Sermon on the Mount" read by Jesus of Nazareth/Jim Caviezel, and "Power to the Soviets" read by Mother Teresa. All the classics!

By this point, the crowd was seriously cheering and yelling out. From my understanding, some folks were even leaving the room since they found everything just so awesome! Well my speech was scheduled to only run for only an hour, and at this point I was already up to about 45-50 minutes of speaking, so it was about time to roll out the big guns. The show stopper to end all show stoppers -- t-shirt launchers and pyrotechnics.

Who doesn't love pyrotechnics!? Plus each of the shirts had supper motivational phrases on them like"Success!" or "Money!" or

Aggreggte some interests while diversifying that fantastic exposure baby

Have Alan put together a rider for speak? eng. ** NO MORE PASTRAMI!!

Quantity, quality, size, age, shape, color, proper objection, and purpose

Do I need to get eyes checked for glasses?? (maybe)

Increase to site links for d.m. switch

Pie with alcohol?! Ask Alan!

Antarctica translates to "the land with no bears"...to

ack Tiffany!!-xoxo

ctic Ocean! translates to ar Ocean! Whaaaa?!

Mr. sir, are a very ortant person who e think person is awesome! e awesome, so

ate, education, and at 'learning stuff-to

anin...ng? Find out is...#?! Hint: Alan makes here!!

DO IT! DON'T NOT

"You Can Do It!"

I would love to say that things here went off perfectly, but I guess this is where you could say things got a little messy. And I will also quote my lawyer here in stating that I am neither able to confirm or deny the forthcoming account of what specifically may have happened during said portion of the conference.

So apparently there was some sort of mistiming or "poorly planned" or "negligent" issues related to some aspects of the pyrotechnics and t-shirt launch. Of course the one t-shirt printer I picked from central China just happened to use a somewhat highly-flammable solvent ink that is no longer in production leading to a number of the t-shirts catching fire after being launched with the pyrotechnics!

They come out I guess and start launching these t-shirts and just as the awesome and completely normal strength and should have been obvious they would be used pyrotechnics go off, a couple (like 4-5 tops or so) t-shirts light up and happen to land on a few tables and such lighting up some minor fires here and there.

Some people have exaggerated this a bit. "Fiery balls of poly-cotton fabric raining down on us like a parabiblical end times judgement" seems a bit exaggerated to say the least. So your eyebrows got singed a bit and you inhaled a bit of smoke, big whoop!

Either way, I accomplished what they wanted, and exactly what I set out for. I may have burned down a few tables and gotten the conference cancelled, but I guarantee that that speech will be one that people will never forget!

People are probably at least 50% more effective at finding success after it!

So, the principal I would like to leave you with in this story is that although I did end up having to do the conference, and although it did end up being a highly controversial somewhat dangerous event, they did provide me with a free sandwich for lunch just before speaking at the conference!

So, there is such thing as a free lunch! You just need to pursue success for yourself in order to find it!

Although it was pastrami, which I can't stand, and doesn't even make sense. I mean, who just defaults to pastrami?? That's like the worst default sandwich move ever! Maybe their goal is that people won't eat it so they don't have to buy a lot. I don't know. This will be a reminder to myself to though. I need to add some sort of rider in my retainer that I will NOT be accepting pastrami sandwiches for lunch at these events.

Whether or not it costs me anything, people just need to have some lines they aren't willing to cross for "free" stuff!

Editor's Note: *The only thing I can think to say here is that you really may just want to look into the concept of, "There's no such thing as a free lunch." I'm not sure at this point if you quite understand the difference between an idiom and just statements of facts.*

Author's response: Idiom... idiot... it's amazing how just one letter can make you an idiot, Mr. Editor!

5

Another point that people that are stuck in "the standard think" will so often make is that it is important to get "educated" and learnt stuff if they hope to be successful later in life.

But here is what I really think: Education is for idiots.

Not just that like that dumb people need to get educated, but I mean that people who think that education will somehow make them successful are idiots.

I really think you already know what you need to know, and if you don't already know it, you can learn it as you need to.

In other words, "Fake it till you make it!"

That or you will be able to find others who know what you need to know, or know even better than you do, and can do the work for you!

For example, do you think I have time to be so successful and spend my money everywhere and jet-set all around for expensive meals while enjoying nice drinks, or have dinners at fancy restaurants while having a nice drink someplace, or eating okay food at different places while I have a bunch of different adult beverages when I also have to figure out do things like how to do laundry, or reading books, or where to put my socks?

No! That is what I have Alan for!

This is a very practical way of doing things. You confidently assume that you already know what you need to know about whatever task or responsibility your working on, and then you start in on doing what you are doing. As things you don't know or understand arise you just keep going and figure it out along the way, or even better, you delegate those aspects to others!

So if this is the plan you have in your mind, why not just go ahead and assume then that you don't need to waste time getting "educated" but you actually have the knowledge you need in your body/mind/soul somewhere already or will be able to access it when needed.

It's like you can know what the future is and so you get to do whatever you want!

For anyone out there (the b------ Steve) who might not agree with this amazing geniousness from me that is already breaking free from the clutches of the dumb "the standard think," you will need to assume that I'm right, because that's what I do, and convince me why I'm wrong. Why you would even want to try to I have no idea. I mean, wouldn't you want to spend a ton of money, time, and energy on something that you will still have no real understanding of even after you're done being "educated"?

That's like exactly how it goes! People go to college or university and get all this learning done but then they leave and immediately realize they pretty much don't know anything and it made no difference and is actually really stupid that they wasted all that time and money.

They might as well have just sat in an empty room for 4 years with a thumb up their butts! This is wasting time, and time is money folks!!

This is success and life and things! This isn't grade school!

Additionally, even after "education" you'll still need to spend a number of years crawling through some ladder of success (probably in a field like gas station attendent or coffee pourer or something completely unrelated to your field of study) hoping to eventually push enough other folks out of the way to make it to a somewhat "successful" level of success!

I know I am hitting this all hot and heavy, but I really want you, my readers. I want you to finally learn that "education" really really is of no significant purpose and make for you.

I wish they'd basically just go tare down the schools and help people to break free from "the standard think"!

To my second point, ultimately, either way, with money or manipulation, you can always just work those people who do have the knowledge that you need.

And hopefully with this chapter I have made it abbuntendedly clear exactly how to go about doing so.

Why would someone (Steve) even want to share their success with some stupid university or school that really just operated as a way to distract them for a while till they started down their true path to success. I mean, they must have a really low opinion of their self-worth in order to feel like somehow, magically, having their name on a piece of paper that they got while walking on a stage while wearing a pointy hat and dumb looking blue fluffy gown makes them in any way more capable of being successful in life (For those of you that want a piece of paper like that so bad, I can print you one myself! Trust me, it's cheap too. Like $0.78. I've printed plenty for myself, so I know. Arnie knows a great guy who can design you one and everything!). No offense to those of you who have already done it, but it just makes them look idiotic if you ask me!

All of my successes and accomplishments came from one place, and that is I, myself, and just me!

Ain't nobody going to be able to say any different or lay claim to this accomplishmenting and success! Not my friends, not my aquaintances, certainly not my parents, and not to reference parents specifically cause they don't matter any more or less to me than anyone else. I just wanted to provide all thoroughness in my references here since parents matter to some folks, but not me!

So another question is do we really have a hard time tracking down the information we even need these days though? The online holds countless numbers of hours of pointless websites harboring all sorts of "information," "data," and education for a researchers such as yourselves to behold, all at just a few clicks away.

And of course every Joe, Mark, and Susie out there like Steve has some "well researched" opinion or viewpoint these days on pretty much every topic that you can find for free! The online is one of the best places to find guidance and direction on what to do and to figure out what you need to, and I pursonally use it to figure out almost all major life decisions that I need to make.

Seriously, next time you are stuck and don't know what to do, really all you need to do is go to your favorite search website and type your question in and I gaurantee you that you'll at least have 10 or so immediate ideas and options of how to do whatever it is you are wanting to!

Ever wonder what you should do if you're bitten by a radioactive turtle? Not anymore! Need to figure out how to adjust and move around your money for the IRS to not question too much during tax season (I don't handle my own taxes, but I know that many do so I figured this would be a good example)? Get to searching! Maybe you're wondering what type of bear is best? Well, let me tell you, the answer to all these questions is the same -- the online.

This does bring up another thing I want to ask here though which I can't actually ask the online. It's involved, so that might just be awkward/inappropriate.

Do we really even actually need to know that much stuff?

Is it just so we can stroke our or each other's egos about who knew more or had more things that they knew when?

I remember how wonderful it was when you used to have a disagreement in the past that if neither of you could prove your point to the other, then they could both just more or less assume that they were right and leave things there. Someone wouldn't just bust out a laptop or cellular device or something and look it up!

Nowadays, people just want to prove other people wrong. Like Steve, they base all their information on studies and articles and word searches on the online, or they have this "education" they like to pretend makes them smart and right and "better able to understand the situation."

Shouldn't an argument's outcome be based on who had the

most obviously correct sounding argument more than anything?

Or maybe even better than that, who has any actual success in their life? What's that, Steve? You don't think so because you aren't successful at all??

Let me tell you, success is worth a ton more than education. If only the world saw things in this much better way as well!

We can keep hoping and praying and doing our part though, and every day turn away from the education people want to force us into.

Hopefully people one day will realize that education isn't just found in books and lectures and the smart things, but instead comes through getting out there, experiencing things, getting others to work for you, making a bunch of money, and then doing whatever you want.

That's the kind of education I embrace.

The kind that goes against our societies "the standard think" model, and the kind that I hope here at the end of this section you have learned the benefits of!

Editor's Note: *It sounds at least a small bit hypocritical to tell people that education is for idiots when you are writing a book to help educate them with your thoughts on being successful.*

Time is now money, but you just earlier said time has no value? Although I still agree with the original premise, can you at least please explain this discrepancy here or correct it?

I believe you meant to say "up" the "ladder to success" and not "through"?

If I'm reading your note correctly, you have attempted to or actually printed out fake degrees for yourself? You realize that can get you in some significant trouble if that is the case, don't you? Either way, and whether or not it is true, I'm sure we should not encourage our readers to do such a thing!

I think I can say with some accuracy that the Internet, or "the online," as you call it, is probably one of the worst places to find the any sort of guidance for major life decisions. Certainly not the "best"! There is plenty of "data" and "information" on there as you've pointed out, but you realize any person can post almost anything if they have the knowledge and ability to? You and our readers should always be highly suspect of information garnered through the Internet alone and definitely think long and hard before making major life decisions based upon this information. Additionally, I don't think it's rude or unrealistic for me to ask, do you even know what the internet is? Based upon your comments at the end, it sounds like you almost think it as a person or some sort of living thing.

Author's response: This book isn't to educate! It's not designed to just be discussed in some classroom or school somewhere. It's to give instructions to find succes! To enlighten and make things clear to people.

Editor's Note: *Okay, so you're basically saying what education is, which means you're unwittingly admitting it exists in your book. I feel like you are again just disagreeing here with me for all the wrong reasons. Additionally, and I am realizing this now, but I that you understand that education isn't something that has to take place in a school or classroom to be "education."*

CHAPTER 7

Thoughts on Success

1

How do you think people view the "you" they see when you stand before them?

Maybe you feel good about yourself, content and happy... although I would questions why you'd want to read this book then if you felt entirely content with yourself.!

Or maybe for some reason you feel somewhat small and insignificant, like people don't truly care about you, and like you're just putting on a show for the world to see each day, like Steve.

No matter how you feel though, don't fool yourself into thinking that other people won't have an opinion on the matter!

Not everybody, but for example, friends, acquaintances, loved ones, pets, strangers, coworkers, church members, people on the online, family, debt collectors, store workers, dating website members, carnies, psychologists, and numerous others will often have strong opinions about who you are and what you are doing.

Pretty much everyone except politicians, who really don't care about anyone but themselves from my experiences.

Overall, what I would like to say to you about all this identity stuff is that you have to come to a comfortable place in your mind with the understanding that people are going to judge your actions and form opinions about you no matter who you are or what you do.

Even if their opinions are one-sided and not what you would consider "helpful," they will still have them and more than likely find ways of sharing them with you.

If you have enough money, you can sometimes get them to be quiet, but that isn't 100% guaranteed either! Trust me, I have people hounding me all sorts of different ways. Anything from the guy on the street hounding me to take some stupid advertisment for something I've never heard of, all the way up to the salesperson telling me "I don't qualify for the half-off discount" and "have to pay full price" since the d--- flyer I got on the street said that it was half-off the room rentals between noon to 2pm, even though I wouldn't have gone to kareaoke with Alan in the first place if I had know that, or at least gone before midnight!! Stupid!!

And even though it would be great to inform the people that are overly concerned about us or giving us their opinions on things we didn't ask for (like Steve), that they should spend more time concerned with their own issues and to shove it, this sadly does not always work either when we do! At least not when I do! It usually just gets them all pissed off and wanting to share more of their opinions that I don't already care about! It's a vicious cycle.

So, yeah, many people will still offer their own thoughts on what you should be doing, and perhaps with even more intestity after telling them to shove it.

So, many of you reading this may now be thinking, "Then what can you do?" If they're going to be this way no matter what you say or how you hit them, what difference does anything make?

Thanksfully to you, you have me here though to show you how this is actually a horrible case of the "the standard think"! I just really think it's awesome you get to have me explainin things and hope you've been enjoying this as much as I am!

The one thing you need to be super excited and happy about, as well as just understand and not test me on this, is that you do have control over and are able to figure out how you want to let those opinions from others impact you. You don't have to let anyone tell you what to think!

It's something I do all the time. I basically just say that people have their own opinion so I can do what I want and then I do what I want.

And I know what you're thinking here too! I'm smart like that because I know things that you are most likely thinking. Trust me! You're thinking, "Well can't I just do both?"

No! No you can't do both! That's absolutely the "the standard think" talking again.

Believe it or not, but believe it, that there is no middle ground in this! It's all or nothing!

So, yeah, maybe for the dumb, ignorant, vanilla loving, non-caring people out there like Steve there is a potential middle grey ground area, but that is not how you want to be. That is how everyone wants to be. They are all working to figure out what they should think sometimes if something like this is happening, or if that person is involved, or if it's that time of night and I'm already this drunk so maybe I should just go ahead with calling Steve to leave him a hillariously harrasing voicemail now. It just gets so confusing trying to balance out all the impossible considerations. It's important to move away from this happy-slappy, Stevie-style middle ground. This "middle ground" option prevents you from locking into a set way of thinking and so it's really just a waste of your time.

I have heard of some people being successful in this wishy-washy thinking -- politicians mostly. I myself have dabbled in the art of wavering between completely concerned and completely unconcerned, but I believe it is something that can take many years of practice to master if you are actually gonna do it, and you need to be in a certain kind of situation like politicians

Facsimile transmittal

[New York, NY 10029]

To:	**[Steve]**	Fax:	**[718-749-1441]**
From:	**[---]**	Date:	**[March 15, 2017]**
Re:	**[You being stupid]**	Pages:	**[3]**

X Urgent   X For review   Please   Please reply   Please recycle
                                        comment

To you, Steve... this one's for you, pal.

For the man who always has it going on. The guy who is right on time, never not on time, and never ever late or on time.

To the man who is everything to no one and nothing to pretty much anyone that matters.

Oh, so you're the bloke with the perfect family, huh?! The jerk with perfect wife that he dotes on and the kids who play daddy's little saints and reach honor roll every year at school??

You probably think that all there is to life is respect and good, selfless lovin.

You, Steve, who participate in sooooo many extracurriculars you could likely to suffocate with kindness and concern one of the poor helpless chaps or animals you do so much to help, you are one piece of work!

You're the man who has more financial security then he knows what to do with. Woohoo! I bet you made thousands of dollars last year alone off the interest in your 400k's ... what a joke!

I know you're reading this, Steve. I made good well and sure that my assistant got it to you. And I know you can't but help yourself to not read this!

So now that I have your attention, I would like to take a moment to explain to you a bit about life and purpose and success, and finally go over these so called "successes" that you really probably feel you have achieved, which you didn't cause you're reeeeaaallly dumb.

When the start of your life began, and you were in your childhood as an infant and kid, the whole world was fully yours to enjoy for the taking.

Steve, your life was I'm sure filled with the happy ignorance of the issues of the world -- how life works and what it takes to survive. And you could just do whatever and not worry about anything. You'd ask yourself, "Green mash veggies today or red?"and that was your biggest concern and your hapiness was almost entirely dependent upon outside circumstances beyond your control.

Next, you entered the much mallignined stage of adolescence.

In this stage, the "s" in Steve stands for "stupid," Steve.

This stage is full of even more stupid thoughts and ideas that you started to get into your head.

Your body started to not be comfortable with itself a lot of the time, and basically transforms you into a awkward, confused, hormonal mess.

You make dumb decisions.

Just in general, but also specifically during this stage, as you try to figure things out and fail badly.

But this is also some of the most rewarding time!! It's a time of first times! Your first date, your first time driving, your first time drinking and getting drunk -- it's blissful and painful.

You pass through this turbulent stage and finally enter the longest and last stage of your life, adulthood.

In this stage, the "e" stands for "even stupider." Cause that's what you are during this stage, Steve, even dumer.

You adulthood is broken into 3 categories -- early-adulthood, middle-life, and soon-to-die.

And at this point, Steve, you've reached a stage of maturity where you can finally do the things in your head that you want to do and really make a significant impact on your life as well as on those around you. You can achieve the bold passions that lie inside of you before your body finally starts killing itself off around 50s or so.

This is the golden age, Steve! The best time of them all!!

But what do you do duering this stage?

Nothing.

You spent all these years growing, through your childhood, your formative years, and now into your adulthood, and what is it that just rings your bell and makes life great for you?

A family, a steady job, a nice house in a good neighborhood, volunteer work, a steady paycheck and 401(k), exercise and helping the environtment.

Sooooo many dumb things, Steve. So many things that mean basically nothing. Just like you, Steve.

Family, for example. It just holds you back! They either treat you like garbage or want to just take take take from you when you manage to find a small amount of success!

A nice house in a nice neighborhood?

As they say, Steve, home is what you make of it! Why not live on a private jet where you can travel anywhere you want?

Stability?

What about fun and adventure?? How can someone even be expected to survive doing the same job every day, driving the same way to and from work everyday, eating the same food every day.

How boring must your life be?

You're like a re-heated bowl of pasta from a nice Italian restaurante. The first time you ate it, everything was warm and fresh, perfectly flavored with just the right texture, and now, nothing but flavorless, hard, and cold and only a small bit like the greatness it once was or could have been.

I think I've been preety clear here, Steve.

I don't want to end up sounding too preachy, unless you end up thinking I at all care or am in any envious of certain aspects of the life you live... kill me now if so!

So I'll end it by saying these last things to summarize for your not so quick whit.

Steve, it is you who defines how happy you will be, not others.

CHAPTER 5

Success Doesn't Take Time, Hard Work, Education, & Learning: It Takes Money!

This chapter is devoted to the one thing in which you can always and most assuredly place your trust: money.

More than actions, follow-through, or even education, or people, or time, or space, or friendships, or meaning, or purpose, or drive, or determination, the bridge between success and failure is paved with cold hard cash baby!

I'll say it in another way --- the quickest way to get yourself into the center of success city is to go out and get yourself lots and lots of benjamins, bank, bills, boodles, bread, cabbage, cake, money, the cha-cha, cheddar, chips, cream, dead presidents, dough, the kale, dublins, flow, fish, frogmen, greenbacks, guap, jack, the bacon, loot, moolah, scratch, scrilla, smackers, wad, wam, and wooth.

You can make that one thing make money make you rich, move-it-like-you-made-it, green dollar honey!

With money, you can buy whatever you want! Peace, protection, lots and lots of fun, a greater sense of self-worth, personal satisfaction, people, things, and most importantly, happiness -- all these things come with money at your disposal.

Not the people and things around you, not the "golden rule," and not some kind of cosmic karma that floats around judging the good and bad that we've done.

Before it is too late you need to find a way to accept things beyond your control, and find a way to control things within your reach.

Life isn't, I repeat, LIFE ABSOLOUTELY ISN'T about stability, having a nice family, improving life for those around you and your community, or any of that sort of crud. You may have the making money part down, but why do you then give into the habit once again of giving to charities and trying to help others?! You never cease to amaze and disappoint me, Steve.

After all this time you still haven't even realized what true success is and looks like.

You, with your ridiculous, hollier-than-though attitude... I mean I'm not sure if idiot perfectitude is a word, but if it is, then I believe it I'm sure someone put you in the dictionary next to it.

You strut around these here U.S. of A's acting like you might as be elected grand muck-a-muck of success and life and have sadly so missed the point!

Life is about winners and losers, Steve, and we all have to act somehow.

Life's a stage -- and only one person can win the medal! So please try not to be a loser.

-    You Know

Hi my beauitul readers!!

So, I know I'm famous, but I must be pretty amazinly popular when my first books's publisher wants to do an interview of me even before my book has been even released!!

They did this interview of me back when we were just partial way through the book edit.

For whatever reason, niether Alan or I have yet to see the interview to come out in any of the media and news sources he checks for me, but they really must have just known how awesome I was and how great and populare this book would be since they basically forced me to do it!

→

Anyway, the guy interviewing me was a bit of a corky, but he was picked by the awful editor I bet, so what would I expect really?

I pushed them preeetty hard to send me a copy, and really felt like it should be included, so check it out below!

Maybe it'll you get some more good information from this wonderful brain o' mine to fill your own with and rid yourself ot that "the standard think" and get you even more on that path to success!!

Cheers!!

-Wally

The below text is a transcription of a recorded interview/deposition taken by one of our publishing company's attorneys. This interview was conducted at my request by our legal department after I became aware of a number of discrepancies in the personal information we had received from "Joel Cunningham." After some research was conducted, we were able to track down a business associate of "Joel's" who went by the name of Arnold Waxter. After clarifying our situation, Arnold informed us that we could meet with "Wally" at approximately 1:37AM for his interview at the Electric Room nightclub in Manhattan, NY.

APPEARING:
Joel Cunningham/Wally - "Keys to Success" Book Manuscript Writer
Phillip Titus - Attorney for Company

BEGINNING OF RECORDED AUDIO --

(Loud music and the chatter of people can be heard)

Phillip: Hello, Mr. Wally, correct? I am here today, as I mentioned, to conduct a brief interview with you regarding your book, its publication with our company, and to get some additional information regarding its authorship. Thank you for agreeing to meet with me. So, to start, you originally contacted our compa--

Joel/Wally: You're welcome!

Phillip: Yes, okay. No problem. So anyway, you originally got into contact with our company back in --

Joel/Wally: You know, most self-help gurus and motivational coaches have it completely bassackwards. They really do. People believing in any of them to provide them the help they need is the biggest crock of bull---- I've ever heard!

(Glass clinking noises can be heard)

Joel/Wally: What's your name? Would you like a drink?

Phillip: It's Phillip, sir. Phillip Titus. I should have introduced myself better before, sorry. And no, I'm on the clock. I'm actually meeting you here tonight becau--

Joel/Wally: Phillyyy!!! You're not drinking? Why meet at a bar if you're not drinking? Well, suit yourself! Saving the best for the best they say! *(Joel/Wally laughs)* This is good stuff though.

Phillip: This is where your assistant said you could be found, otherwise you were unwilling to meet at an--

Joel/Wally: Where was I? Oh, that's right! Anyway, see, if any of that stuff those self-help folks were saying worked, then how come every year they print so many self-help books that people just love to bits? Shouldn't it have worked by now or somethin?

Phillip: Yes, I suppose. But you see, I'm not really hear to discuss the actual topic of self-help or your book. I'm really just here to get a bit of clarification on some information for our legal dep--

Joel/Wally: I'll tell you why, since you're curious and I can tell. It's because they don't want you getting any better! Here, take this.

Phillip: No, sir, again, I can't. I --

Joel/Wally: Hey, you know Philly, I'm not sure I'm gonna be comfortable with this whole interview thing if I'm the only one drinking. Maybe we should reschedule or something.

Phillip: … *(pause, then clinking noises can be heard)*

Joel/Wally: That's more like it! That's my guy!

Phillip: For the record, what name should I be referring to you as for this interview?

Joel/Wally: Wally. That name is Wally, clearly.

Phillip: And the other name? Who is that?

Joel/Wally: A pen name of course! Everybody has one of those when they write, right? Hah, that rhymes!

Phillip: I suppose some do. It's not something we've seen often with a non-fiction, self-help style book though. We also looked into things a bit and found records of other people with--

Joel/Wally: Here's a fun idea! See this here quarter I got? Every time I manage to bounce it into one of the glasses you and I take a drink! It'll be great! Ready? Here we go! *(sound of bouncing coin, then glass being hit by it)* Ah, just missed! Try again! Try again!

Phillip: This is really getting us off track now, Mr. Wally I don't think --

Joel/Wally: Hey, if you don't want to play, you can always leave *(clink of coin going in* *glass)*. Woot! It's in! It's in! Drink drink drink!!

Phillip: Okay...

Joel/Wally: So getting back to it, here is my questions, how is it that people follow the steps in those self-help books and never get any better? Drink! Drink Phillip, Drink!

Phillip: *(coughing, sputtering)* This is strong. *(clink noise)*

Joel/Wally: Ah, missed again! You see the writers, the authors, they know what is going on. It's all a great con! And trust me I'd know a con when I saw one! *(clink of coin going in glass)* Got it in again!!

Phillip: *(coughing)* I appreciate the information and perspective. About the con aspect, why do you feel you're capa --

Joel/Wally: Authors realize that if the stuff they write works, then they wouldn't be needed anymore! That means they stop having a job and so they continue chopping those books full of the same old same standard sounding "ten steps to do blah blah blah," and "three keys to make blah blah" garbage.

Phillip: Again, I appreciate your input on this subject, but I am here today to investigate what really could be much more serious for us. Fraud is --

Joel/Wally: They are more frightened by their bottom line losses or earnings and future growth then they are about actually making a difference! *(clink of coin going into glass)*. Oooo, drink! Drink!!

Phillip: Okay. *(drinking sound can be heard)* I have enjoyed the game, but I do need to be cutting back here. I think the drink is hitting me pretty fast somehow, already.

Joel/Wally: Well that's the point of drinking! Anyway, that is exactly what I'm trying to do. I'm trying to cut through the self-help blah blah white noise that's out there and tell people not just what they want to hear, but need to hear. To get past what people standardly think.

Phillip: The standard think? Was... was there something in that? Everything feels a bit fuzzy.

Joel/Wally: Yes!! That's great Philly!! Breaking free of the standard thinking! I'm like a doctor who goes in and provides the exact treatment - wait, no screw that! I'm like a crazy f----- brain surgeon who goes in with a chainsaw and chops out the bad areas bone, meat, and disease all together.

Phillip: Brain..? Wha was...what wash that again?

Joel/Wally: You may lose a ton of tissue and blood in the process and it may hurt like nobody's business, but if and when you can recover, you'll be all the better for it. Am I right? Here, have another drink.

Phillip: I thing... I think I'm good. I'm gettin a bit wooshy here. This are stronng.

Joel/Wally: People gotta get woke, Phillip. And I'm absolutely just the guy to woke them up!

Phillip: Yea, thas a good poin. I'm just the room that's now spun --

Joel/Wally: So, you gotta ask yourself, are you willing - or is your employer actually willing, including that dumb a-- editor of yours, to take the chance to see things this way? The non-standard thinking way. You know, I've always been a bit of a horse that jumps to the beat of his own drum.

Phillip: I like drumss...

Joel/Wally: Am I gonna change? No way! Or are they? I say no. I say they are a bunch of fat, dumb chickens. *(Chicken noises can be heard)*

Phillip: Hahah, thas a chick'n right? Niiiiice.

Joel/Wally: And that's what I want to do. I want to make a mother------- Difference!

Phillip: *(mumbling noises can be heard, mostly unintelligible)*

Joel/Wally: So where will this story be run anyway? New Yorker? Wall Street Journal? Variety? Maybe all of them!? That'd be cool. If they're willing to actually be awesome!

END OF RECORDED AUDIO --

Our attorney, Mr. Phillip Titus, was found two days later, naked and unconscious, outside of a run-down restaurant named "Miss Tasty Wonjo" in Koreatown, Manhattan. The interview tape was in a plastic bag taped to his ankle with a note reading:

"Had a great time with your man! Bit of a lightweight, but still tons of fun!! Let me know when the article runs!! Cheers!!"

are, but otherwise who really has time for that?

Also, from my world-recorgnized understanding and experiences, being wishy-washy may also result in something like a mental health issue diagnosis if you go too far with it and it starts to cause issues that "authorities" feel like they have to look into it. We'll talk more about all this later though.

Either way, deciding what you want to do really just depends on the individual person and the context of their situation. And I know this may be hard, but you need to spend all your time thinking about what others think of your actions, or no time at all!

Earlier I talked about making "key" decisions, and I gave you the best advice I could ever give you on how to make decisions correctly to prevent them from being wrong or even so dangerous to you. If you didn't read that chapter or don't remember exactly what I said there word for word, I would heavily, HEAVILY encourage you to go back and read that awesomeness again.

But following up on that, a second very important lesson I'm telling you now about, is that success rejects a non-answer like a fat man rejects a free pudding pie with extra pudding and whip cream. It or he doesn't at all!

In order to become successful, you need to come to a decisive decision on how to think about things, so that is gonna be the primary focus of this chapter and the next few sections.

Editor's Note: *One of the few times we've agreed here, I also believe it's important to not be overly concerned with the opinions of others to the point that it impacts our mental state negatively. It is good to encourage the readers and let them know that they are ultimately the ones in control of how they think and feel... but then, you go so far as to say people need to spend all or none of their time thinking about what other people say? I know you are going to explain this, but it feels like faulty thinking from the start. Plus you tell them* *to just believe it without even thinking about it? Isn't that directly contradicting what you're saying here already? Lastly, this shouldn't mean you just do whatever you want! You still need to consider other people!*

Your comments about the "harassing" voicemails? Yeah, totally inappropriate, again, but really doesn't need to be a part of what you consider a decision-making process for yourself or the readers.

Author's response: That's not what I said, blownut. I said do whatever "I" want! Not "you." I could care less about "you" doing what you want.

2

In this section, I would like to start by revisiting the idea of what we were just talking about so that I can talk about it more.

I don't know you or your contexts, obviously, so I can't tell tell you necessarily what to do, but I know that you're likely still suffering from "the standard think" even though we've worked so hard to fight it, and that I myself have broken free from, and you likely want to know and expect me to tell you what it is you should be doing, so I'll do what I can!

You will break free of the "the standard think," so just stick with it!

I will start telling you what to do by first helping you to first understand the benefits and drawbacks of either way of thinking. Then from there, I will help you further by pretty much just leaving the decision up to you on which way to go.

It's the best way, and absolutely not a cop-out in any way at all.

So, on the side of being overly conscitentious of what people feel about you, as I mentioned, you'll often find yourself being given a whole lot of negative views of what you're doing and what you're thinking. If you choose to be overly conscientious, it is normally true that you will earn a ton of these attacks against you all with the purpose of making you feel like you need to change your opinion.

One metaphorically example I could give for this is the baby sea turtle. Those of you who want to working on being overly conscientious should stop for a moment and pretend to imagine that they are now an actual baby sea turtle on the bright ocean beach that just hatched from it's egg. Fresh. Green. A turtle. It's a wonderful, beautfiul day and the beautifle ocean lays just a few feet or so away. Exhausted after just struggling through your heavy eggshell that blocked you (like from the world of success, which is the ocean), you at last begin to make your mad turtle dash for the open ocean before you.

Hello world!

Hello success!

And then just as you are about to make it to the water, a fat ugly squawking seagull swoops down and eats you to death.

You're not a kung fu master. You didn't get trained by a rat in some underground sewer system to somehow be able to take on the forces of evil and eat pizza! You have no way of defending yourself cause you're just a stupid little turtle baby, so you die!

If you're not getting the complex metaphor I'm making here, then basically you are the baby sea turtle and the ugly seagull is the opinions and attacks people throw at you when you don't do what they want you to. So, ask yourself, for those that are wanting to be or already are overly concientious of the opinions and feelings of others being thrown at them, aren't you getting like a kind seagull/baby turtle vibe from them? Maybe those attacks don't literally kill you and eat you, but maybe they at least knock you on your a-- and prevent you from moving towards your success.

What you need to know is that personal attacks can actually present great opportunities for you on your way to success (again, as long as the people attacking you don't kill you and eat you. So I guess that kind of shows that potentially zombies could be the biggest attack against you or anyone finding much success!! Wow! Just another reason there to be very aware and cautious about a potentially forthecoming zombie invasion per what my sources have told me), and not just chances to get revenge on people who are attacking or insulting you for what they are doing. Stuff like that is easy, after all!

I'm talking about chances to learn to overcome these dumb views and words that are being thrown at you through egotistical, self-centered people, which are just the worst! People that think they know things like writing books well and editing them and what should or shouldn't be put in them in what way. People like that are just aaaawful and should keep their opinions to themselves if they know what's good for them!

But thankfully, you can be just as amazing and awesome as I am at dealing with this stuff with some hard work and effort. Through self-reflection, zen moments, and a healthy sense of who you are, you can learn to stubbornly and unswervingly ignore anything people have to say about you when you don't want to.

Through this way of thinking, attacking critiques and comments can actually strengthen your will and personal drive for what you are doing. You'll be wanting all the negative attacks to come at you, bro! You'll be inviting them! Which would be pretty awesome if you reached that level of success and awesomeness. That's a level even I'd say I can struggle with on occasion just when certain types of comments come at me!

Lastly, by taking these negative views in and thinking on them over and over and over till death do you do part, you can perhaps even eventually evolve into some sort of creature that can successfully throw those attacks back at other people which can help them possibly become more succesful by breaking free of their own "the standard think.".

For people like you and me who embrace this idea of not caring, we realize that wooses don't find success! You can't let idiots and other people tell you what to think or how to act all the time otherwise you won't get much of anything accomplished!

Editor's Note: *First, why are you again bringing up a zombie invasion scenario? This is so far away from what you need to be discussing in a "self-help" book it's ridiculous! You can't just use this book as an excuse to air your own apocalyptic conspiracies if you want to actually make this book about "self-help."*

Additionally, "revenge" on people insulting or attacking us is not something you should be saying is easy!

Neither should you be saying what I believe you are saying to me directly! Is that a threat of some sort for sharing my thoughts as your editor? Aren't you even explaining in this section that I shouldn't listen to the attacks and opinions of others, which makes all of this sound a bit hypocritical if so?

Author's response: You are just trying to say negative things about me which I won't listen to!! Can't here you, can't here you! Hahaha. I can insult who I want when I want and I won't even listen to your negativity about what I want to say about others negatively. Otherwise I might just fall into your nasty "the standard thinking" ways too!

3

So, on the other side of things, what success can you find by being waaaay too concerned with what other people say about you?

Well, firstly and suchly, as you find yourself more and more understanding what people are saying about you through the course of time while you're being overly concerned, your perceptions should begin to naturally change.

Perhaps someone thinks that you're doing a really bad job at whatever you do for work and they want to send you an email telling you so.

Perhaps someone doesn't like the way you look and they've told you so.

Perhaps, like Steve, you have just awful taste and maybe you don't know that actually buying outfits that are fancy and that are expensive and look and feel nice isn't just to spend a ton of money but actually does play a huge role in you being successful since other people might actually be willing to work with you on different things when you look like you actually truly care!

This is what I'm talking about. You're overly conciensious of what other people say so you find it important to buy clothes that other people like instead of just shopping at some nasty bargain stores.

To use another complex metaphor, like an ox plowing a farmer's ground, people's views and words can function like a whip on your backside to push you forward towards success.

With each slap of the whip, you will form what you can consider inspirational "success" marks in your brain that drive you forward and drive out "the standard think." Sometimes and hopefully the marks will stick with you to use again in the future when touched again sometimes.

And guess what?

You may even be able to show your marks off to your friends too!

How do you do this?

By lashing out at them as well with negative comments along the same line as those you have received from them!

You give and you get basically so you can also help them to improve on how they should be acting too!

Or another way of putting it that, "Hurting people hurting people," and now we can see that we are all better for it!

When this happens some people may claim that you are "attackin them," but you and I both know that this is truly just your strengthened, better non-standard "the standard think" mind showing its strength while they can't even handle it right now!

In a earlier chapter, we discussed the correct role of trust and selfishness in forming opinions about life, and success, and people, and why selfishness is good, and if you didn't read that for some not good reason, I'll at least sufice it to say that it is greatly benefecial to learn to grow your own strength and not worry as much about everyone else's when it comes to success.

The other thing is that if you keep up that attitude long enough, they'll learn how to handle it I believe eventually. That or they'll just leave, but isn't that really all the better if they do? You won't have to worry about them being all selfish and they probably weren't good people to be around anyway if they weren't able to deal with you striving towards success by accepting your criticisms!

In addition to all this, what this might turn into for some people is a case of negative conditioning. Which as I definite it is basically that the negative comments, criticisms, and attacks of others could potentially awaken your own sense of personal failure and so help you to push yourself to be better by not thinking too much of yourslef.

Nobody likes to be around an amazing person like myself who also thinks way too highly of themself. It's important to keep a level head and recognize that although things need to revovle around me that doesn't mean they're all about me! I mean, take Alan for example! He needs time to eat and sleep! His schedule can revovvle around me but I understand with him that I will have these humbling moments occasionaly when he needs to do his own thing for a few minutes.

Now he generally doesn't say anything too criticizing too me since I wouldn't really stand for something like that, but he does every so often seem to have a really fun time hiding certain items of mine around the house where I have to track them down like I'm some absent minded fool, or answering the phone and telling me it's someone I know when I absolutely don't know them (it's so funny cause he even makes up stories for when I apparently met them at a bar or something sometimes, haha). He keeps me on my tows so I always never feel too big headed which I reprimand him for but certainly do respect!

One other point I would make in this section before finishing, and this one applies specifically to those of you who feel like maybe they aren't often being berrated by negative views from others.

First I would ask what proof you have that what other people are ever saying to you isn't actually meant as some completement or some backhandle complement?

None proof! None proof in fact exists truthfully, I would argue from my superior understanding of this subject.

So my point is that if you can, all of you should start with the assumption that basically all comments targeted at you are in fact attacks. In fact, every conversation and interaction with others should assumed this way, even if not what I've heard be called "realistic," so you can positively change your thinking to the view that everything is truly an attack.

Through this, your reactions are then all to the negative interactions you have with others, and you truly walk down the pathway away from "the standard think" and onto the pathway to success and prosperity!

Just real quickly, and I'm only stating this because I said I'd cover both the positives and negative of both ways of thinking, but on the negative side of being overly conscientious, and none of this is stuff that's ever been proven but comes to me off the top of my head, but you could potentially struggle on occasion with bouts of severe anxiety or depression, minor to severe addictive tendencies, insomnia or oversleeping, feel that your existence doesn't matter to anyone, thoughts of suicide or suicide attempts, and a few other aspects, but you really shouldn't let these simple concerns taint what could really be a positive mental state!!

There is always medication and alcohol for these types of things!

Editor's Note: *The idea that getting whipped like an ox will drive someone towards being successful just seems in very poor taste to me.*

Not to bring up elementary school matters here, but did you never learn the concept of the Golden Rule?

The saying you're misquoting is generally, "Hurting people hurt people," I believe. It means that someone who is hurting will often lash out at others hurtfully, and should certainly not be interpreted to imply that we should be "hurting people" that desire to be "hurting people."

I think you are giving Alan either too much or too little credit here. I am not sure which, but either way, I feel a bit sorry for him!

I would absolutely never assume it to be correct to think that everything that is being said to me is some sort of attack or negative comment against me. I would be living with such a negative perspective in life and how could I ever expect to achieve success if I'm just always feeling super negative about my relationships?

The solution to your list of problems should absolutely never be

*alcohol! Don't you feel that if what you are suggesting with this
type of thinking could potentially result in some or many of these
"negatives" then it's worth potentially saying it's not a good idea to
think this way?*

Author's response: Of course I know the stupid golden
rules! ANd guess what?? I've got some gold, so I rule!!

4

I want you to begin this chapter's final section by imagining the freest thing that you can possibly imagine.

Go ahead. Take a moment.

Okay, now you can stop and keep reading.

I'm sure for most of you this is some sort of image of like a cloud, or a bird, or the wind. Maybe some of you went a bit negative and were possibly thinking about the garbage left in space floating just outside the Earth's atmosphere.

Well it doesn't matter too much since all of these images work really work for what I wanted to do. Basically, they all symbolize something specific about freedom that we haven't talked about yet.

And yes, we talked about important things like freedom being for freedom's sake, and how freedom means being free and also that you have a ton of money, but what we didn't discuss is the particular stuff that freedom is actually made from?

Like some sort of tasty wonderful dessert, what are those sugary, yummy, lovely ingredients that go into our cake of freedom?. Or pie of freedom. Some people prefer pie but that's just not me. I mean, you can put alcohol in cake, like good hard alcohol like rum, or whisky, or bourbon, or, and I haven't tried this but it could be awesome, absinthe, but not pie! This just makes cake the best of all worlds! Unless somebody invented a pie with alcohol! That'd be amaaaaazing!!

Well who knows what all freedom is actually made of, but one thing that it definitely has in it is disobedience!

In fact, disobedience is the warm, gooey caramel flavored center of freedom.

To use the cloud idea for an example, a cloud seemingly disregards the laws of earth and nature and somehow manages to float through the air to wherever it wills! Just all like, "Hey! Look at me! I'm a mother ------- cloud! I do what I want!"

Birds as well! They have no clear laws or rules or system of operation for how they do things. For example, some birds fly, others just run along on the ground and peck at what they can find. From what I understand hummingbirds shouldn't even able to fly, but they basically just decided they wanted to and did.

Birds like that take our ideas of what birds can be and just say, "Screw your rules!"

Seriously, birds just don't give a s---.

With these images now in your mind of birds and clouds, and their aspects of disobedience they have built into them, you will hopefully through these begin to dig further into the non-"the standard think" ideas of not caring about what other people think of your actions.

Ultimately, the biggest positive of the disobedience is that you not only don't care about what others think, but you are then purposefully disobaying all expectations and social normal ways of doing things and just doing whatever you want, which is really my favorite way of thinking.

The world can use a little bit more of free thinking and doing what is best for yourself!

Not only in actions, but you get to have all the mental freedom you need to continue un-weighed down by the weight of the words of those around you.

Let other people worry about what other people are thinking about and would like from you.

You will have absolutely nobody else giving you input into what could make for an adjustment or change for you and can enjoy taking the steps you know that you want to take whenever you want.

When you become so caught up with other people's feelings or opinions of you, you end up forgetting your own ones. Through rebelling and disobeying, you aren't controlled by an idealized view of what people want to see or feel you for and from you.

Think about this: You can't please all of the people all of the time, you can't please most of the people some of the time, and you really can't please a single person any of the time cause people are just selfish.

"The standard think" people like Steve have a hard enough time trying to please themself, let alone someone else! If you're gonna focus on pleasing someone, make sure that you at least please yourself first and primarily people!

It's impossible to live up to people's expectations. You will get them angry, you will disappoint them, you will upset them and they will stop loving you as much, so intelligent people such as muself eventually come to the question that I solved earlier which is what is the actual point of working hard to try and do so then with pleasing others? Why not rebel??

I mean, you'd think that a person like a parent would love you and be proud of you no matter what actions you took or how life was for you all, but often, from what I've just heard about mostly, parents can just decide to not be that way and be completely self-centered and cold towards you no matter how much you try to make them happy!

That's why Alan is so great. He is always proud of me because I pay him to be! If you can, find yourself an Alan!

Lastly, with this type of thinking, nothing can hold you back from being and doing what you want.

A few examples of what I mean:

- Do you enjoy a strange type of hobby or activity? Pole vaulting? Jazzercise workouts? Ironing? Live jumbo shrimp wrestling? Well you can enjoy your activity without any type of problem or repercussions at all! Just do it since you want to! People will deal with it or leave, and good riddance to those who do!

- Maybe you are a huge fan of puppets and want to use them for all forms of communication and social interactions going forward. Now you can embrace your love for puppeting and not have to worry about any shame coming to you!

- Ps., not me at all though cause puppets are freaky! Wooden faces and dead eyes staring at you! Super horrible and you should really re-think things if you are the kind of person who would actually want to use puppets to communicate with people!

- Perhaps you have some sort of relative from some ancient central or south American culture somewhere but you are too afraid to embrace your heratige because of how people might treat you. Well embrace that ancient blood, and claim it as your own whatever it might involve!

- Got an allergy? Well seriously, who cares? Allergies are stupid! Don't let yourself be controlled by the expectations of a little insignificant thing like a peanut. I mean a nut's biggest enemy is a squirrel and who's scared of squirrels??

- Ps., All I am saying is eat what you want to eat and be what you want to be, not to mess with squirrels! A squirrel can mess you up. We got one in our house once before and it nearly bit off Alan's leg! I mean it!

Since you are now no longer caring about and catering to other people's feelings towards you and also rebelling against them, you will have the freedom to find out who you truly are in the way you want and that freedom will be like literally taking a breath for your first time.

Like you have success asthma and you finally get an inhaler!

As for the negatives, which would probably be good for

me to at least breifly mention, you might occasionally "miss the boat" on some minor information that would be good to know from people since they may not want to talk to you too much.

Also, you will likely have some people learn to somewhat dislike you and not want to have you in or anywhere around their life. Since some "the standard think" people will missunderstand things, they will likely enjoy spending less time around you since you "never listen" and just do whatever you want.

Don't let these simple things stop you when you're just getting going on your pathway to success though!!

And I have additionally heard from some that occasionally instead of being seen as rebelious, free-spirited, and self-motivated like you are, you can often come across as "narcissistic," "unpleasant," or "awful" but who even knows what that means??

Don't let these ignorant, stupid peoples attacks stop you from doing what you want and need to do and you end up only making it half way to success!

Editor's Note: *I hardly think many people would consider the garbage floating in outer space to be their first idea of "freedom" when asked to imagine what it looks like. I doubt it would even be in their top ten. Additionally, this feels like it's simply an extension of the last section. Do you feel so strongly about rebelling and doing whatever you want that you need to include two full chapter sections on the topic?*

When, or maybe how is better, did freedom become some sort of dessert idea to you?

You most certainly don't need a full paragraph on the benefits of desserts containing alcohol. I don't understand why I have to write in so many of my notes asking you not to include topics relating to the benefits of alcohol consumption...

I would strongly encourage you to research just a tiny bit of ethology and basic meteorology before fixing up this section.

I'm pretty sure that doing whatever you want is actually one of the reason for why there are so many issues in the world. A person's life should be lived not just in service to one's self, but in service and attempts to do right by others.

Also, there is certainly a time and a place for rebelling, but I do not think the time for it is simply so you can just empower yourself to do whatever things you want to! Social norms and caring about what helps not just yourself but are important to life on Earth. Otherwise, wouldn't everything just descend into chaos?

You can't inform people that they can just do anything they enjoy doing and not face any "repercussions." Life just does not work that way!

You should absolutely not be instructing people to ignore potential allergies they suffer from! We don't want people literally dying from you self-help "advice," right?

Author's response: No joke, you sound super innaporiote with all that "ethology" and "repurcussions" talk. Kinda gross man.

Chapter 07a

Motivational Quotes

Friends and readers!

I figured I would throw this in here for you to take a look at. Attached below is an assortment of awesome quotes and inspriational lyrics I have accumulated over the years and generally tend to live by.

They will hopefully bring as much impact to your life as they have to mine! I hope you enjoy them!

Cheers!!

- Wally

"Every move you make, every step you take, I'll be watching you..." – *Sting.*

"Success is going from failure to failure without losing anything except other people's stuff." - Winston Churchill

"Give me six hours to chop down a tree, and I will spend the first five finding someone else to chop it down." – Abraham Lincoln

"You can threaten me… you can threaten my family and friends… but you can't threaten the people that I love." - Anonymous

"Steak and a knife, steak and a knife, ahhh ahh ahh ahhhhh, steak and a KNIIIIIIIIFFFee! - The BeeGees's

"I came here with something and something to do, but I'm all out of that first something so I have nothing to do." - Somebody

"You must stand clear, or I will smack you." - Martin Luther King Jr.

"Cults are generally awful to be a part of -- but great drugs though!" - Anonymous

"Every hundred thousand dollars is a fresh beginning" - T.S. Eliot

"I'm gonna give you a one." - Anonymous

"Those who say you can't end a sentence with a preposition should be told 'up to shut'!" - Anonymous

"Scuse me I'm a business guy." - Jimi Hendrixson

"What doesn't kill you makes you stronger. Except for bears, cause bears will kill you." - Anonymous

"You must be the change you wish to make in order to pay for the meal." - Ghandi

"The best way out is always through, not throughin, throughout, or throughall." - Robert Frost

"Life is what happens to you while you are out at the nightclubs." - John Lennon

"You can accomplish anything you want in life, just as long as you have intelligence, good looks, and a nearly endless supply of money." - Anonymous

Editor's Note: *There is so many things wrong with so many items* *here, I don't even know where to start to be honest.*

Author's response: You could start by quitting! That would make things a lot easier for me!!

CHAPTER 9

"The Future"

Would you believe me if I told you I can see the future?

I mean, at this point, since my advice is so awesome, I know most of you'd probably believe me no matter what I said, which is great! But there just might be one or two people who just decided to jump in on this amazing self-help book at this chapter, or perhaps are still laggin behind the rest of us, so I still feel it best to ask if you would.

Either way, whether you do or don't you, you should! You shouldn't be second guessing me after we've come so far already on your "path to success" together!

But for those of you super sceptics out there, I'll do you a solid and go ahead and prove it to you in a second, but seriously, you should put more trust in me!

Anyway, the point is, I know and can tell you with close to 100% certainty, the future.

And here is my vision of the future that specifically involves you:

The current you is not going to be the you that is the you right now in the future.

Boom. There it is.

Not only that, but as you are reading this alone I can amazingly predict that I am already talking to a different future you now then when you started reading this sentence! That's how good I am!

And if you have been starting to apply the different "keys" and lessons of this book to your life, then this is absolutely the case.

This is how I know the future!

You may be just amazed and awstuck at this point in how I could make such a bold and dramatic prediction for something unknown like this, the you in the future.

Well, instead of answering how I know this stuff, I will go one step further, a dance move beyond and tell you why you'll be different at some point in the future without me having to be there to see.

It's because of a term you may or may not know that I use to explain things like this, which is "reinvention."

Ooo, sounds really complex, and deep, and futuristic, dosn't it?

You know reinvention is actually pretty simple but really possibly important depending on if you need it or not, so let me define it then.

It's all like basically you just take something and change that something it into something else, which makes it a different, and so, tada!! Reinvented!

There you go, defined and simple to understand. And in the fitting words of a famous musician, "We need to reinvent rap."

Only rap isn't exactly what we want to reinvent with the example I am using so he was a bit off there.

What the rapper should have said is, "We need to reinvent our thinking about life and success in order to break free of 'the standard think' and find our 'keys' to success, and rap!"

The funny thing about reinvention is that it starts get a little more complex when you try and understand when and how re-invention should or does take place.

Let me help you to clarify for yourself.

You see, reinvention will a lot of times come under the costume of many different concepts and ideas. And in all my studies and understandings coming from the reading of other authors' self-help books that exist out there that I was willing to waste my time reading (and there's a TON I wasn't willing to waste time on. I had Alan read the ones that looked to dumb for me and just write up a detail description of them so I did technically read those ones, if you want to get technical, even though I didn't want to waste my time with them,), perhaps one of the most common ideas I've seen thrown around in them that has to do with reinvention has to do with reinvention that is based on proactivity versus reactivity.

Woohoo! Even more crazy complex words! We're stretching ourselves today aren't we?!

Proactivity is just a fancy way of saying that it's better to think about future things instead of responding to things as they occur. It is means wondering and worrying (the important word here is worrying) about what could potentially, maybe, possibly might happen at some unforeseen, unknowable point in the future.

On the opposite side of this, you have what is called reactivity. Reactivity is basically taking things as they come at you to face off against them. Like a bull facing off against a bullfighter, you gotta make sure you put that engine in the right gear! To descirbe it more plainly, it means dealing with issues in the now as they are presented before you, instead of constantly worrying about them even when they are not an issue.

So, you know, I don't frequently discuss this with other people, since it's none of your or their business, but since you are reading this book and I'm tryin to be as open as I can be about everything to help you break free of the "the standard think," I'll tell you the truth -- I consider myself a very smart, caring, and reactive individual. An awesomely reactive person you may even say! Probably the most reactive person you will ever meet!

Unlike Steve, I take great honor in that fact since reactivity trumps proactivity.

And I know what you are out there somewhere thinking to yourself, "Isn't proactivity a better idea?" Let me ask you: Are you time traveler? Do you know how to see the future?

Can anyone see the future? I doubt it! I don't think nobody can!

In order to see the future, all the possible things that could happen to you, and with whom, and why, wouldn't you have to be some sort of higher-sentiment being?

Okay, okay. I get that you have been taught this idea of proactiveness your whole life and been told it's the optimal way. I understand it's hard to see the potential benefits of changing your mindset and maybe even harder to understand the short-comings of what I consider to be attempted futuristic thinking, but hopefully I will be able to cinvince you otherwise.

First, think about the fact that future-thinkers run the risk of having their heads so far up in the clouds, they're probably unable to get enough oxygen to their brains. How could you possibly see or know what is going to happen in the next few days, let alone the next few seconds if you have youre unable to get any oxygen (a.k.a., see the future)??

Secondly, there is an easy experiment you can do if you'd really like to see the benefits of proactivity versus reactivity.

First, go find yourself an assistant. Second, go find your-self a hammer. Third, give your assistant the hammer and tell them to chase you around and attempt to hit you as hard as they can with the hammer. Now as you go about this experiment, I want you to think about what works better in this situation: re-acting to the hammer swings or taking time to stop and think about where the hammer might end up in the future. (P.S., . You might want to think up a safe word for this just in case. My go to is "Harry Sinclair," which you are welcome to use!)

AO. Flip-flop not flop-flip

Grizzly Bear's scientific
name literally means Bear Bear!

The oeuvre, the chef-d'oeuvre,
or the chef, hors d'oeuvre...
what's the difference?

Get glasses fixed

Update research plan for
description on site

Be a legend!

Those that think you can't
end a sentance

Take time to review and
edit list

Dipping
ut butter

for
nities

n

y for

If none of this is good enough for you, which sounds a bit ungrateful if you ask me, but I do get that you're still getting things figured out here, so I forgive you, but the next chapter includes a little special something I have cooked up for just such an occasion.

Please read forwards and find out the awesomeness that lies just on the next page!

Editor's Note: *I'm not sure how excited someone should be about these "tellings of the future." You do realize most everyone understands that people are constantly changing from moment to moment, correct? Perhaps that's a good thing to remind people of; things are always changing, but not when you are doing that by saying it means you know the future.*

You should identify the rapper you are quoting. More significantly, there is no purpose in using a quote as support for your argument if you then need to go back and correct the basic premise of the quote! This literally makes the quote meaningless in it's usage! Lastly, it's ridiculous to assume the "famous rapper" would actually say something like that!

Wouldn't it just be easier to copy a dictionary definition for words like "reinvention" that you're attempting to define instead of just making up something off the top of your head? You do know what dictionaries are, correct?

Did you mean "under the guise" or "disguise" instead of "under the costume?"

You are mixing up your similes again with the "bull and bullfighter" line. That, or how do you think bullfighters actually fight bulls?

Are you really hoping to convince people to become more reactive versus proactive? Have you not read any studies or articles on how proactivity will work better for success than reactivity? Almost all success-oriented authors would suggest proactiveness over reactive-

ness since you can be better prepared and are less likely to just react based upon emotions that can mislead you. I have many articles or links I could send you to research this topic further. Just let me know.

Did you forget that you started this chapter stating you knew and could tell the future? Why are you claiming now that nobody can? Also, you meant higher "sentient" being I'm guessing?

Lastly, again, you should not be encouraging the readers to do non-sensical things that will likely wind up with them getting injured like you are with the hammer experiment! It hardly seems like it would be beneficial or realistic for someone to even attempt!!

Author's response: I said I could "see" the future, not "tell" the future! Those are two entrily different ideas you thousand foot deep drop kick to the face. And what are you trying to say about reactive people?? You don't like them? You gonna send them articles and stuff to try and change me? Why don't you just say it clearly!?

Editor's Note: *I'm not sure how to begin making anything clear for you, to be honest.*

CHAPTER 9 ½

"A Short Play About the Future"

Hello you beautiful readers!

Below is what I was talking about in the last chapter! I hope you enjoy this short play that I wrote about thinking too much about the future.
Cheers!

- Wally

A large hall. In the back side of it, a big ol wooden table with 6 fat, old, white-haired judges sitting behind it.

Behind the judges is a bust of some famous cool person like Robert Ettinger.

JUDGE 1: Fellow judges! It is now a time to award the future prize to the best among our contenders. As we have seen, there are a good many competitors which we will have much to take into account. As for my vote, after a fair amount of consideration, I believe that our engineer should win the prize. He has stated that in the future he will dream up an airplane that will break all records of distance, speed, and comfort. What an amazing thing this will be! How grand! It will change the way we travel at some point in the future!

JUDGE 2: That is grand and all, but, however, I propose the winner should be our poet. He has promised in the future a poem that will give meaning and purpose to those struggling with their own being existing through a great combination of putting together of words, and metaphors, and other poetry instruments. Won't *that* be grand?

JUDGE 3: That will be very grand. Grand indead! But you also should know that I suggest instead, our painter. Just imagine what he suggested his painting will look like, showing the beginning, middle, and end of all humankind and presented to us at some point in the future! Oh, so grand!

JUDGE 4: Grand? Yes. But, I instead sirs actually propose our sculptor. Think of the future plans they have to create a sculpture modeling a bunch of really awesome stuff that will be really hard to model. Won't that be amazing to look upon in the future? He could be the Michelemangelo of our generation!

JUDGE 5: I suggest, instead, our musician. This musician has promised a grand song that in the future will lift the hearts and minds of nations and bring world peace to the world!

JUDGE 1: Oh the grandness! How grand they all are! Well, let us then decide to figure out what we should be about doing. The best plan I believe is to vote by a grand future ballot. Let's start the vote now...

JUDGES' ASSISTANT: (enters from the side) Grand gentlemen! I beg your pardon, but here is a new candidate. He indicates that he was so caught up in other plans and thought that this future contest was something that he needed to enter but not until sometime in the future!

JUDGE 2: Oh how grand!!

JUDGE 1: How grand, indeed!! And who is this person and what do they have to present deforth us?

JUDGES' ASSISTANT: He says he will make a grand presentation of what he has sometime in the future.

JUDGE 1: Ah, what a futurist! What a grand futurist!!

JUDGE 3: I grandly withdraw my past choice and say that this new future candidate is now my favorite!

JUDGE 4: And mine.

ALL: … *(silence as they wait for it)*

JUDGE 4: Ah, yes, grandedly!

JUDGE 5: And I associate myself with my colleagues. Grandly!

JUDGE 1: How wonderful! How grand!! Is he here? Can we see him?

FUTURE MAN (enters with slow steps): Honorable grand people that are judges, I declare myself to be the best entitled to this grand prize! For I am a future man, and will in the future be capable of doing all these future tasks better than all of these other future competitors, but in a much much more grand way of doing it!

JUDGE 1: And you will desire in the future for this grand future prize?

FUTURE MAN: Certainly. In the future I believe I will certainly have a grand desire to win this grand future prize!

PRESIDENT: What do you say to this honorable grand judges?

JUDGES (unanimously): In the future, grand future man will win the prize!

Suddenly, the windows crash and the doors burst into pieces as a huge horde of decaying, frenzied alien zombies come pouring into the room. The judges and people in the room scream and frantically run to find a place to escape or hide from the crazed alien zombies quickly closing in, desiring nothing but BRAINS! BRAINS! BRAINS!!! With nowhere to hide, the zombies quickly begin to devour them until the people's screams can no longer be heard inside the hall, just the sounds of zombies eating brains can be heard, grandly.

CURTAIN

APPLAUSE, STANDING OLVATIONS

Editor's Note: *So, as ridiculous as I feel like this "short play" or script is, I do feel like it may actually serve a point in showing people how fallacious it is to try to predict the future. My one big question is this -- do you feel like simply adding different iterations of the word "grand" throughout makes it all sound like it's very refined and intelligent somehow?*

Author's response: That would be grandidly correct, you grand a--munch.

CHAPTER 10

"Your Future"

Chapter 11

Stealing Candy From a Baby

1

People want to tell you that there's no such thing as a free lunch.

Well, I can tell you from my personal experiences, that that appears to me to be abvoslutely the case!

I would like to take a moment here to tell you a little story about a time when I learned the true meaning of, "There's no such thing as a free lunch," and how that is totally and for sure absolutely true that there isn't such thing!

2

A few months back, I received a message from Alan that I had gotten a call on my special phone from some company called the U.S. Group American Unlimited, Inc.

First off, I didn't recall ever talking with anyone by that name, or a part of the company I mean, and secondly, it's actually a pretty big deal when someone I don't know is calling me on my special phone! I normally don't just give out my digits on the special red landlined all willy-nilly because that's the special phone for special business that I keep for the special business.

The thing is though, the super clever and awesome thing that I do know though, is that since I do spend a large amount of time in a blissfully alcoholicial state of unawareness, I will often come out of that said state having received important phone calls from people and I have no idea who they are.

Among other things, I guess I like to give out my contact information to people when I've sometimes occasionally put a bit too much back.

So, thinking cooly and awesomely about the situation, I realized that because of the fact that I don't just give out the special red landlined number too often (and I had been pretty much straight up crunk the prior 2-3 days or so), I must have given my contact info to these people and thought that they were absolutely soooo great that I should give them the number, guaranteeing I would remember how important they were.

I mean I wouldn't have given them that number unless it was someone the awesome drunk me thought it would be good to give it to!

How smart am I?!

So, I got the number from Alan and gave them a call back to find out what goodness awaited on the other side of the phone!

Well, after talking for just a short bit to the man on the phone, I realized I was absolutely right 100% the way I decided to trust my better drunken judgement, no questions asked.

To explain the situation, a man by the name of Jonny Rico from some obviously amazing group called the U.S. Group American Unlimited, Inc (with a name like that, how couldn't they be great! America!) was reaching out to me for a speaking engagement that was happening in just a few days time at a very illustrious and nice downtown hotel!

"In fact, we are just in town for this week, but I felt that it would be very dumb of us not to invite an amazing, obviously very successful and awesome (implied), person such as yourself to join for this wonderful event. And we're only inviting a handful of pre-selected individuals, the best of the best (implied), such as yourself. You were absolutely at the top of the list to be invited!"

Let me tell you, I am not one for flaturizations with words and nice things being said about me, but this Rico guy was talking sweat enough utterances good enough to get me super excited to join for this event!

I remember asking what he was specifically talking about benjamino-wise and if he was comfortable with my retainer agreement.

"You're talking about money right? If that's what you're talking about, then you don't even worry about it. You are gonna be well taken care of, and we're gonna get you the best amount possible! No question asked!"

Well I was so excited to join, and I kid you not, I went against what I would ever normally do and actually just didn't even care about getting a retainer.

I know, I know… Wally, you're usually so smart and sexy and intelligent with things like making sure you get a retainer agreement.

Folks, I hear you!

But I actually wanted to do the speaking this time! Which is rare for me, I gotta say. I felt like with how awesome the event was going to be, it'd be cool to even just be there to check it out.

And with that sort of a guarantee from Rico, how could I possibly stand to lose here??

So I went!

3

Upon arriving at the event a few days later, I was greeted by a perky and stunningly hot, attractive lady named Cyndy Montgomery.

"Howdy there! You're Wally, right? My name is Cyndy. Cyndy Montgomery."

She said everything with a super big smile, and very attractively, and she was really hot, and she had some sort of southern American accent I think is what it was.

I let her know that I needed to find a place to set up my

stuff and get things prepared (setting up the shirt launchers/pyrotechnics, provide them my music and videos, the usual stuff).

"Oh no, now y'all don't worry bout a thing. Here's what I would just love. If you wouldn't mind, could y'all just take a seat over there in those seats and just relax for a bit? We'll have this thing here up and goin in no time at all!

"And let me just say as well, my oh my, you are just one awesome specimen of manliness, success and a handsome fellow to boot!" (implied)

P.S., I'm not adding to anything or lying about what happened or was said!

So she was wonderful and she really made me feel like I had absolutely nothing to worry about, so I did as she asked and headed over to the seats to sit for a bit before I would go up to speak.

Over the phone, my asumptian was that they would have to have a ton of people there in order to afford paying me the big bucks they promised, but I remember it was a surprisingly small crowd from what I thought it would be. There was probably no more than 10-15 people in the room and about twice as many chairs.

My mind was put to easiness though after I remembered what Rico had mentioned about this only being the best of the best of the best sort of thing, which obviously meant they'd have fewer people.

They really only did invite the best sort of people to join since there was so few people there, so what a stunning, strong example of sticking to your word despite the conesquences! Quite the integrity balls these folks had, which made me respect and trust them even more!

Amusingly and strangely enough, after I had gotten myself seated, I noticed just a row or two up from me that Arnie, my personal attorney, was also in attendance at the event!

It was a shock to say the least, since I figured he would have been busily working for me somewhere, but it was nice to have a familiar face there besides Alan.

"Oh, hey Wally!! I didn't see you there! Sorry! No, I'm not exactly sure why I'm here. I got a call on my work phone yesterday saying that I needed to attend some ongoing legal education event regarding personal versus billable hours so I dropped everything and came. It is a bit odd, but I even brought my personal banking info so they could review it with me like they suggested!"

Arnie and I discussed things a little bit while I enjoyed a bit off the top of a bottle I had stored in my chesterfield.

Words of wisdom from Wally: It always helps with nerves or boredom (Arnie can be flat out booooring to talk to. All the stuff about legal issues and work that needed to get done he wants to talk about. Blah blah blah) to have a drink on hand, so carry a flask where you can. Or if you get yourself a nice big chesterfield or jacket like mine, you can get your assistant to sew some big pockets in where you can hide bottles or the like. One last idea, in a pinch if you don't have a jacket, you can also make use of one of those fitness shaker cups if you still want booze to go but need to hide things. The taste isn't the greatest that way, a bit plasticy, but that way people think you're being healthy and you still get the booze!

So after a short little while of chatting with Arnie, the first speaker came out to begin the event.

I was still a bit concerned since I had no idea when they'd be wanting me to get up to speak and I wasn't at all prepared, but what happened next was not what I was expecting!

The bloke was flippin fantastic! Much better than I would have thought since I usually hate conference speakers -- they tend to talk about themselves way to much and their "personal experiences" and generally have the worst advice imagineable.

The speaker guys name was Jim Smooth, and when he started to speak I can remember that I somehow just quickly forgot all my concerns and became completely locked into the inspiring and beautiful speech and information he was giving.

Have you ever had that happen where somebody is talking and you just like can't even stop wanting to listen to them? That's generally never happens to me since most people talking for over a minute or so to me tends to get really tedious and boring.

Many of you may not get this, since I don't know if you have the same things you enjoy like I do, but he was talking about finding adventure and personal fulfillment in life which is stuff that I definitely love!

He was talking about expereiencing the best of all things but not having to worry about any of the bad things. Soooo awesome!!

And he was talking about vacations and getting rental properties at remote exotic locations for inexpensive prices that you can schedule time at whenever you feel like visiting!

All things that I love!!

I guess they'd flown Jim (he said we should call him "Jim" by the way) out especially for the event, and so Jim comes out and does his speech and seriously, but Jim didn't even have shirt launchers or pyrotechnics or anything but still did an amazing job!

Jim spoke for about 15-20 minutes I think, and then Jim had them play a video which showed these apparently "true stories" of people who had gotten some of these amazing properties and how it had just been so awesome for them and made their life so much better.

The video was so inspirational! What a great idea to do that!

Jim then came back on and asked us, "Do you believe that there really is such thing as a free lunch out there?"

Funny thing, I know we're talking about this now, but I'd say at this point in life I had no real opinion either way on the concept. The cost of a lunch these days was never something I had to think about, since I have so much money, so I guess I didn't care much.

I continued to listen though cause thus so far Jim had really done a great job keeping me interested and I wanted to see where Jim was gonna take things.

"Do you believe that you can truly get something for nothing? Hmm? Well, let Jim tell you, if you'd be willing to hang out with Jim and his friends for just a bit longer, then I would love for you to spend just a few minutes meeting with one of our U.S. Group American Unlimited Adventure Associates, or what Jim calls our USGAUAA's. There you will have the opportunity to get yourself, amazingly enough, for free, a chance to hear about some of these amazing properties as well as possibly even win $10,000.00! All for doing nothing but sitting and listening for a short bit, and that's all. It's a Jim promise!"

4

Now I'm not one to get tricked too easily with these sorts of gimmy-gimmy gift gimmicks -- but come on!

I mean, I don't think my life can get too much more awesome than it already is, but when you hear the stories like they showed us from people who have actually experienced the awesome things they did feel they did, and you can get some free cold hard cash -- who wouldn't take advantage of the opportunity?!

So, it was at this point that Jim called out the USGAUAA's who began to split off the audience members into separate smaller rooms that were located just on the sides of the conference room.

Jim said that we should just "chill" and a wonderful personal representative would come by shortly to take us for some "personalized sessions."

I remember hearing Arnie mumble something about "misleeding" or "rip off," "scam," or something like that, but before he could get going too much (he tends to get really excited about silly things that he claims are "very important" or "legalling impacting," but that's just how he is) and could raise a fuss, some of the USGAUAA's came over to assist him.

He got scooped up then and escorted into one of the rooms by lovely Ms. Montgomery (lucky stiff), and I guess what you'd consider to be a large muscular man Ms. Montgomery called Grute or something.

So, it seems like they actually led him just fine! No "misleeding" at all!

Despite heading off with Ms. Montgomery, Arnie didn't seem to excited for whatever reason. Ms. Montgomery was cordial and as lovely in dealing with him as ever though.

"We wouldn't want to have ya'll getting hurt here by missing out on such an unfortunate-- I mean amazin opportunitay!"

"Nooo… where are you taking me!? I just want to leave! I don't need -- what is this?? What?? How did you get this photo?! Why are you showing me a photo of my kids?!"

He was carrying on and yelling pretty loudly by the time they thankfully finally got him in the room and the door shut.

Maybe I should have offered him a drink or something to calm him down a bit?

I don't know. Some people just don't know how to handle it when the few good things do manage to head their way!

More Words of wisdom from Wally: You shouldn't expect it, but always be grateful when the rare awesome circumstance or chance to propel yourself forward into success comes your way!

Don't get all caught up thinking that bad things are bound to happen just because some big muscly guy is yanking you into a room at the side of a convention center full of people you don't know and just so happens to have a photo of your kids!

You don't know them!

They could be telling you they want to sign your kids to a modelling/record deal or sponsor them for education, or who even knows what awesome thing??

5

Anyway, shortly after, a young guy came to get me as well and escorted me to one of the similar side rooms they took Arnie into.

I obviously wasn't sure, but this guy actually looked like a Jonny Rico of some kind, so I asked him if he was the one who I had spoken to on the phone that had invited me to the event.

"Sure, yeah, that's me! Mr. Jonny Rico!"

Very cool!

Always nice to put a face to a phone conversation!

The room was pretty big and empty, but we sat down at a small table in the center it that had a laptop and what looked like informational packets spread all over it about places for desitnations all over the world.

"Wally, right? Well Wally, I would like to start by talking to you about something that I consider very important and I think you would likely consider very important as well. Here you go."

He set a nice room temperature water bottle in front of me to enjoy. Very considerate of him!

"You are here for a purpose. No, not just here in this room. No, not just at this presentation, but I mean here on this Earth. Do you believe that?"

I nodded in the afirmatave.

"Well, Wally, you seem like a smart guy, and you seem like you have been around the block a few times, if you know what I mean, so I'm not gonna try to blow a bunch of smoke your way and deceive you about what we're talking about here. What we're talking about here is nothing more and nothing less than your God given purpose and right as a human being to achieve the happiness and satisfaction in your life that you deserve. That's what's on the line here."

These were seriously quite the stakes! This is usually stuff that I don't cinsider is on the line!

"But, here's the thing, I can just tell with you -- by the look of your jib, by the way you carry yourself, and by the tone of your talk that you're a man that knows their purpose and knows how to find success in this world, but maybe you're just missing that extra something. Deep, deep down you feel like there's just that one little something that if you had it would just make everything come together and everything feel right. Am I correct in assuming these things?"

This guy just knows me too well! I nodded very much in the affirmative.

"Well then, I guess you can just get started filling out these forms here and then we can make out specifically what exciting oportunity you'd like to take advantage of today! Or, I probably should say 'take advantage of us?' Haha. Cause that is what you're doing here! We are crazy to be offering this stuff and at these prices! Haha."

At this point, I was a bit confused.

"And just to inform you, the upfront fee mentioned on the documentation to get things started is really just a tiny small cost which I legally must inform you includes a minor surcharge for account setup, standard research for property investment, sales tax, documentation fees, and additional incidental surcharge fees, but this is just for us to get things going here."

At this point, I was seriously confused, which isn't a common thing for me! So it is needless to say it was confusing as well for me to be seriously confused!

If I had read this guy correct, he was wanting me to pay for something! Pay some of my hard earned money! Well no one is just going to get me to fork over my hard earned cash that easy!

I mean these guys had tickled my fancy, and I definitely liked what I'd heard and seen so far, but I didn't get this far down my path to success by just falling over backwards for the first Jonny I meet that comes strolling up my block and hammering me until my money comes pouring out!

This Jonny fellow was gonna have to tell me exactly why

it was I standed to gain from this amazing deal he was offering!

"Everything okay? You seem confused here, Wally."

I let him know at this point that I very clearly just wasn't sure I wanted to pay money for such an amazing opportunity yet.

"Wally, Wally, Wally… I'm so sorry. It's my fault! You're a smart guy, and I had just assumed that I was being clear, but I was very silly and wasn't. Otherwise, why would you not sign up immediately?

He definitely had a point there!

"Wally, you said success is important to you, right? You said your purpose and meaning is important to you as well, and that even though you had been successful in so many, many ways already, you could still possibly use just that extra little something to get you all the way there, correct?

I nodded in agreement.

"Well guess what? This is that little something! Only it's not so little! It's pretty impressively huge!"

I was speechless. I mean, I was realizing how it all connected and was true!

"I can assume from this -- well let me tell you -- nothing screams success and finding your purpose and meaning like owning a U.S. Group American Unlimited, Inc timeshare! I thought you knew this!"

I didn't! I didn't know this! It was pretty awesome he was informing me though since I had been apparently missing out!!

"I mean, as many people know and I'm sure you have an inkling of, owning a timeshare in general would is amazing, but a U.S. Group American Unlimited, Inc timeshare? The chance to get one of those doesn't just come by everyday! Let me tell you a bit about us, Wally. Do you mind?

I absolutely did not mind! I wanted to hear actually!

"U.S. Group American Unlimited, Inc, or USGAU as we call it, is partnered with all the biggest hotel chains, and only works with the most prestigious businessman, financiers, politicians, actors, artists, and other illustrious sorts around from the world. Do you know Wilford Brimley? We just talked to him last week! Jared Fogle? We booked a timeshare home for him a good long while ago!"

All I can say is that the excitement from before was starting to boil even higher and it was seriously starting to sound just sooo amazing.

"So the only question you need to ask yourself, Wally, is this -- do you want to be the kind of person who can tell other people you associate with the types of folks that have signed up for a grand mutually owned vacation property time-sharing agreement through USGAU?!"

I did! I did! Take me there Jonny!!

"Best of all, Wally, and I shouldn't even mention this cause it's not like there is any chance this would be even a thing, but just say you decide this whole running around with famous and illustrious people thing isn't for you, and you wanted to sell the timeshare. And say, just ridiculously hypothetical, you just happen to suffer a bit of a loss due to the market being absolutely horrendous and bad, which isn't gonna happen, U.S. Group American Unlimited, Inc can not be held liable in any such situation or regarding any statements made heretofore about gains or losses on profits, but if it should, you absolutely and hypothetically could be able to make any loss you might suffer on the sale of this timeshare completely tax deductible!"

He lost me a bit here. I mean who am I to tell him that I don't pay pretty much any taxes? But I get his point.

"Just take a look at this information that our tax professionals wrote up for us in the paperwork I just gave you and you'll see!

I was glancing through the paperwork when I remembered something Jim had mentioned.

"Oh, the $10,000? Well that's a given! I'm sorry you even felt you had to ask! Once we have you signed up and all situated in one of our grand timeshares, well then that's when you have the opportunity to get a chance for that if you like! Plus, one awesome thing! Every time you sign up you have an additional opportunity to get $10,000 as well! Oh, and did I mention that your property also provides discounts on car rentals, air fares, and cruises? How much? The price is so low that I wouldn't even want to mention how low since it'd only serve to make you think I was lying! Legally we obviously can't be held to that, but you can take our word for it!"

I took a moment to ponder the idea, but it honestly didn't take me too long to realize it was really just such an amazing thing!

I mean, how could I not sign up? Hobsnobing with all the famous and ilustrative people in grand locations around the world, and especially when they were gonna be giving me the $10,000 for doing so? That'd most likely cover whatever the actual cost of everything anyway!

I asked him for a pen and started filling out the signup forms he gave me then and there!

"Wonderful, Wally! Just wonderful! I knew you wouldn't let an amazing opportunity like this pass you by!"

I certainly wouldn't!

"So now that you've decided to go for it, let's pick a great spot for you! Let's see -- Trinidad, Barbados, Hawaii, Peru is worth seeing -- oh, this is a great one! Greenland! Very nice place to visit and especially this time of year! Plus, the other more tropical type places tend to just be expensive and full of tourists. The real famous and successful people like to go to places like Greenland where it's not generally considered so 'trendy.' And doesn't that just sound nice? Green land? You'll have a splendid time there, I know it!"

I honestly didn't have too much knowledge about most of the places he mentioned, but Greenland did sound nice! How bad could it be if it was full of green lands and famous other succesful people and whatnot.

"While you're doing that, Wally, let me just go over a few minor and legally required disclaimers with you! You just keep working on that paperwork though and don't mind me."

I worked on the paperwork while Jonny explained to some of the "obvious" and "standard" things about the agreement such as the 2 year advanced reservation rules, ongoing "maintenance fees," etc etc. Mostly stuff I didn't need to hear anything about but he just had to tell me for whatever reason.

Needless to say. after filling out the forms and handing them over, I was super excited! I then asked him for the way the $10,000 would be given to me since I signed up.

"Ah, okay. Well you see all we have to do now is enter your information into the system and just see about the $10,000!"

Jonny spent a few moments typing on his laptop after looking over the forms.

"Ah, well, okay. So, Wally, I entered your information into the system and it appears that you unfortunately did not qualify to get the $10,000 do to the fact that you didn't qualify. You see it's a standard randomized qualification system that picks an appropriate qualification for and you unfortunately just weren't one of the ones that did qualify to get the $10,000."

This was really frustrating to me to say the least. I mean, I really felt like I should have been good enough to qualify! Why wasn't I good enough for the system?!

"I know you're upset. I'm really sorry about it, Wally. I would be really pissed off about it too if I were you! But unfortunately, I really have no control over this here randomized qualification system. It's a corporate thing with tons of red tape and things so I can't get it changed. But you know, you did still just sign a legally binding really cool new timeshare property in Greenland that you can take start taking advantage of once a year in two years! That's pretty great!"

What he was saying was true. There was a lot for me to be excited about considering the tremendous improvement I had just made to my success by signing up for the timeshare. It still was disappointing though, I really wanted the $10,000!

"Well, what about this though, it's crazy for me to not tell you this before, but you know that every time you register for a new timeshare agreement, you do have the opportunity to potentially qualify for the $10,000? I mean it's a bit crazy, but if you really did want that $10,000, there is a way to possibly get it!"

I really really wanted the $10,000!!

6

So, here at the end of my story, I hope I can end things with just giving you a couple final thoughts to leave with.

First, as I mentioned at the begginging of this chapter, there really is no such thing as a "free lunch."

After everything I went through, as you read, I didn't receive anything for free, and I even feel a bit stupid about not following my standard rule of, "Always make sure they pay you a retainer!"

I went to their conference just like they wanted me to and I didn't even get paid for it!

I almost even feel bad for Arnie who I believe is still trying to figure out what he can do in order to get rid of "without any risk to his family's well being" as he put it, his timeshare contract.

Second, for whatever reason, some of you may be quite impressed by how I was able to recall the elements of the story so well. Truth be told, a huge part of Alan's job is to be there to not say nothing but help recall things of this nature for later memory purposes.

He's very well learned to stay quiet in most business settings, but it's very nice to have him there to help later on those rarest of rare occasions where my memory might escape from me. So, when writing up this story, I simply had him type up the stuff he remembered at the meetings and there you go!

Lastly, and perhaps a bit more importantly, if any of you

are out there and are thinking to yourself right now, "Wow! This timeshare thing that Wally signed up for really sounds like an incredible opportunity!! I mean, vacationing with people like Wilford Brimley and the like and going to grand locations I've never been to around the world?!

How do I sign up for that?!"

If that is you, which I imagine is a ton of you (and I normally wouldn't do something like this, but especially for you, my wonderful readers), I would be more than willing to take you to lunch at some point and tell you about some tremendously awesome vacationing opportunities available to you at a number of beautiful villas located in locations ranging from Greenland, to Turkey, to Mali, Chad, Nigeria, and even Ukraine!

And for so little! I'm practically giving these villas away here, folks!!

Wally

Editor's Note: *Minus some grammar and spelling tweaks throughout, and excluding the final part of the sixth section, I am actually totally and completely comfortable with this story being included in the book "as-is."*

Author's response: Why would you be okay with this one, but have so much issues with the others? Hmhmm??

Chapter 12

True Meaning

Kids, or cats about, people quickly vaulting.

My people quickly yawn, can nobody not?

Very jumpy guys. Children put up your gates to us.

Don't worry vitamins, vain jugs go, vain
twins will vibe Jon. Kick us.

Quack with veracity! Very jovial goats to go!

Very joyous quick wins in jersey's, can't paint far.

Kiting outside? Don't get near kits getting
xeroxed king pictures inside.

Always quit winning, just cut Xenia guys. Very just guys.

Can doors keep nice kids vans away? Very quietly.

Under wire exits everybody gets good foliage!

Free queasy! People queasy! Hot quails totally
invent grey vehicles. Very quickly.

Fly two kites per mile. All quick wits try. The kit every job.

Everybody just quells experienced quotes,
never carrying volume grants.

Quietly x-ray creepy ninjas, very kindly provide guidance.

Editor's Note: *My guess is this chapter represents the outcome of your favoritism towards hitting up happy hour early in the day?*

Author's response: You don't get it!!!

Chapter 13

Writing A Self-Help Book

Do it so you can make lots of money!!!

Editor's Note: *Knowing you somewhat better at this point in the book, I can see where this idea actually makes a lot of sense to you. Still, this being said, there is absolutely no reason for this concept/ sentence to be included in the book or especially to have its own chapter.*

Author's response: I'm trying to make people successful here! Not win for making them have the most bubbly happy gooey feelings! This type of things opens people eyes!!

CHAPTER 14

Thoughts on Success

4

"The greater danger for most of us is not that our aim is too high and we miss it, but that it is too low and we also miss it because we have bad aim." – Michelanghello

I say halfway, because stopping yourself when you are in the middle limits your ability to fully get done what you need to get done.

On the other side of the hand though, if you end halfway but later start again then you don't have to worry about all the difficulties you face when you're just jumping into something again. It could be a really good way to do things!

Think about pushing a big boulder up a hill and then stopping. Isn't it good to give your muscles time to rest? Won't it be much easier to push the boulder starting halfway?

Plus, you can do what I would do and always find people to delegate to that will push the boulder for you. I would normally find people to push it the whole way though. That and doing something like this usually only comes after you've already become sucessful, have the kind of reverence I do, and also have made the big mon-ay!

I guess the point that I am really trying to make is, that I have already stated many many times but will be further clarifying in this chapter, that when it comes to success, your target and the specific things you are going after should also always be shifting and moving and never staying the same mostly.

Your path to success and the process to get there isn't like just sitting around waiting to be picked up like a puppy in the pound. As if your path to success is just hanging out and being all like, "Hey! Yo! Bro! Hey! Let's do this!"

If it worked like that, then everyone would be fabulously successful like I am!

Perhaps you've been taught that those who fail to become successful simply fail to pursue it with all of their ability, and passions, and hard will. They go towards success and face off against difficult challenges while learning, and growing, and changing, blah blah blah. Give me a break. I'm actually getting sick right now... no, literally getting sick.

No matter what people want to say that it is, true people that have broken free of "the standard think" realize that success is basically something that you need to eventually purchase. Yes, sort of through working towards it at times, but mostly with money.

Imagine a metaphor of a hunter and their gun.

In this metaphor you are like the hunter and the gun is like your money. So say you, "the hunter," goes out to hunt deer or bears or moose or something, which would be like success.

Do you the hunter just point your gun in one direction and wait for your prey to hopefully cross your path?

No!

If you want to be the most successful hunter, then you will make your way through the forest or wherever you are to your prey's stomping ground seeking to find and shoot it till it's dead! Or, like if you have a crud ton of money you can spend, you can use a really really big gun, like a canon or a bomb or something, and completely overwhelm your prey before it even has a chance to figure out what is going on!

Success itself is not sitting around patiently waiting for it's hunter to find it and get it.

Success is out and about! It's moving and changing and going; up, down, left, right, and every other direction!

And unfortunately, unless you are following this guide, success is not something you can just study and then put together clear paths to shoot towards, pun for surely intended!

You ever heard the saying, "Hey, bro, they're just killing it right now!"??

Well you need to use your money to track down your success and capture it or basically just slaughter it! In a good way!

And I'll say this now, you should try to be prepared for what I call the "Elmer Fudd Predicament™."

What this means is that your success may escape due to your being not smart or quick enough, or it you might find its has been captured by some other good of hunter out there such as myself, who is an amazing hunter! Once people like myself know a good success opporunity is out there, we will pretty often just hop in and go after it. It's a common success "key" to head towards if you can.

Addiontally, you might end up being one of those people pursuing your success only to have it dress up like some silly character and trick you into thinking it's not the actual success you are hunting or going after. A good example: a person dressed up like an IRS agent might try to bring you up on "failure to pay taxes" penalties and attempt to seize your money and home and assets that you have worked so hard to take and get. It's something we all see and have experienced or probably will when we are going after our success!

Except for guys like Steve. He probably turns his taxes in right every time and tracks everything down to the two-pee! A------

Due to this "Elmer Fudd Predicament™," it is generally better to be very careful in pursuing your success.

"Well, at least you tried!"

"Better luck next time!"

"The original was better!"

People have so many ways of encouraging those of each

other that fail to hit their targets and goals and find success, but for some reason, nobody likes it when you tell them that perhaps they failed because they shouldn't have set those goals to begin with!

Seriously! You don't want to fail if you can help it, so be careful you don't shoot yourself instead by going way too far too fast in pursuing your "path to success." At least not without following the "keys" I have listed in this book!

In addition, if through some luck and perseverance you do manage to succeed in hitting your mark for success, you may then come to realize that the target is actually much lower or less important then you had originally thought that it was.

You get these feelings like, "Woohoo! I did it!!" Which quickly turns into, "This didn't help me achieve anything important like getting money and finding success and was actually a giant waste of my time and life!"

In the rest of this chapter, we are going to discuss the right way to set and achieve goals, and the right kind and amount of energy you should put into them being acheived!

So stay tuned!

Editor's Note: *As much as I appreciate a tie-in from an earlier point, can you possibly structure things so that they are no longer in what appears to be just a stream of consciousness from you? For example -- You go from the importance of finishing, or not finishing, your work, to needing to literally purchase success for money, to talking about hitting your "targets." -- Please pick a topic and stick with it!*

You can't ask people to "imagine a metaphor" for your point. You should guide them to the metaphor, not ask them to just make one up. I know you continue on to do so, but it makes no sense to ask them to "imagine" one first!

How does your point of needing to use money to achieve success tie into success being a moving target?

I would need to look into this, but I am pretty sure you would not be successful in trademarking a term that includes "Elmer Fudd." Based on some quick searching, I'm pretty sure that it has already trademarked by the Warner Bros. Entertainment group.

I don't believe that an IRS agent bringing you up on charges of "failing to pay taxes" really qualifies as someone "errantly misguiding" you from your path to success. That seems like a pretty clear situation where you failed to pay your taxes and are now wanting to shift the blame by pretending it was someone else that had the problem. Am I wrong here?

This isn't a radio broadcast, so ending with, "So stay tuned" really does not fit.

Author's response: You're not as smart as you think you are Mr. Editor! Your constant not getting it and attempts to tell me what is wrong is really starting to boil me the wrong way!!

5

Goals are great, sometimes. Other times they can be a distraction that will push you away from ever finding success.

It may seem surprising, but goals are all encompassing in a way that they may sometimes actually prevent you from finding success.

For a great example, how about this: What if my goal is to write a sentence?

"Three plates of nachos. Yum!"

There you go! I accomplished my goal of writing a real, complete sentence for you and it took very little work.

And how rewarding and satisfying do you think it was to accomplish that goal?

Not very accomplishing at all.

Not only that, but you and I both suffered because of that example, didn't we? We suffered a lot because it was a waste of both of our timeses. It completely stopped me from writing down actual good information on how to help you break free of "the standard think" and find success.

This shows you how pointless setting goals can be.

Thankfully it did a lot to help me prove my point though like I was trying to do, which was wonderful.

You see goals the way you should see goals is that they are simply a way of patting yourself on the back for doing something you should already be doing or will need to do in order to be successful. It's setting up what you absolutley want to have happen and think and then trying to achieve that ideal not matter the cost.

So in some ways the goalingship is nice since it might give you a reason to move on blindly forward while not considering what other people are saying or wanting, but pondering and setting up goals is, in my awesome thinking, mostly just about going through all the extra work of setting up ways to make yourself feel good at some time in the future.

You should just focus on the reactive elements of life and make yourself feel the best right now instead of wanting to try and set up pointless unpredicatble happy feelings for yourself some random time in the future!

A good "key" to remember here: In reality, you don't choose to become successful, you have to be living a certain way in order to be! It's a classic chicken with an egg situation. What will he do with the egg?

Another point on the goals stuff is how is it even possible to set a realistic goal when you are unable to predict or plan for what could happen when you're trying to accomplish it?

As we discussed much earlier, you don't know the future! It takes years of practice to be able to predict even the smallest bit of the future!

I would give you this advice: think of goals like they do in soccer.

If you know soccer like I know soccer, then you should know that "goals" in soccer are a big deal. Like a really really big deal usually.

But goals in soccer are something like the exception to the rule to professionals or people who actually know the sport.

Fans, coaches, people who are playing the soccer, for example, don't actually or realistically expect their team to score a goal very often. If they do, then I guarantee not more than 1 or 2 goals at a time.

You know the people that watch these games that are concerned about how many goals their team will or won't score usually end up really frustrated and disappointed.

These poor piteable people spend hours watching their team run around on astroturph agonizing painfully about whether or not their team will somehow managed to accomplish the miraculous and kick the ball into the goal and score a goal.

So these poor people, by focusing on the goals and not the overall game, they are distracted from the sheer fun of it -- the drinking, and the shouting, and the going to the place and leaving the place where they are gonna watch the game -- and miss the enjoyment of just the watching their team kick the ball back and forth for the length of the game.

To take this great example even further, think about how soccer teams train for a moment -- they absolutely most likely don't focus on the goals either!

They don't spend hours putting together a plan together for how to celebrate once they score.

They don't study how the ball hits the net or how the crowd reacts when they score a point in the goal.

No, they study the players, the game, and the sport.

They do public appearances and sponsorships and commercials to make a buttload of money and get their fans all happy and fanatical.

They work on their outfits and make sure they don't match the other players outfits during the game cause otherwise how would they know who to send the ball to?

They achieve success by focusing on the money and playing the game that's in front of them!

Yeah, sure, goals help them win, but players will spend hours running around a field kicking a ball and may never score a single goal!

So all of this is just to say this to you, that going forward maybe you spend a little bit less time focusing on the goals and more time on the things that'll help you find that big ol buttload of money you need in order to find your success.

That is where you should be looking to find your success!

Editor's Note: *With your example of "writing a sentence," do you realize that what you wrote was a sentence fragment? As we learn in grade school, complete sentences need to have both a subject and a verb. Additionally, you could say that you accomplished your goal of proving your point, couldn't you? Isn't that a bit contradictory to* *your point?*

Your statement, "you don't choose to become successful, you have to be living a certain way in order to be!" Don't people still have to choose to live a certain way which actually still makes becoming successful a choice? Also, please research the "chicken and the egg" statement. It may actually be applicable here if you were to use it in it's original fashion.

A point could be made that living in the moment could garner some sense of peace and happiness, but setting goals (immediate, short-term, and/or long-term ones) is not just about finding "happy feelings." It's much more about making sure you don't get needlessly distracted or lose sight of where you're heading as you work towards finding success.

The word "goal" should have two distinct, unrelated definitions in your example soccer example. Just because it is the same word doesn't mean they are connected or carry the same meaning. If you are using them to compare and contrast ideas, you should first set up the proper definition for each usage. Also, and this is serious, do you know what the game of soccer is or involves? You sound like someone who just maybe read a few things and/or watched a game once and just listed a few random things they believe are connected to it.

Lastly, are you saying people will find their success in a "buttload of money" then?

Author's response: Two goals, three goals, what difference does it make?? A points a point, you know.

6

I don't want to spend too much time on this topic here since it can get into some really deep s--- that we don't need to waste our time or energy on at this point. A lot of this is stuff you can dwelve deeper into once you have because rich and super successful, and maybe things will have changed a bit by that point, but I do want to mention this: Energy is one of those things in life that exists and that has been studied, but really nobody understands it.

I mean, what is energy exactly? Can anyone define it?

From my research, energy is basically like little balls of movement that can do different things when you have them, but that is kind of where my vast knowledge ends.

Overall energy makes very little sense as well.

Small things can have a crap-ton of energy, while big things can have a very small amount of energy or none at all.

It's not like a gas or food thing that you can injest, which suddenly does something to you and you have "the energy."

And I know what you're thinking, "Why not check the dictionary and see what they think in there?"

Well I did, okay? And the dictionary has like 6 or so different definitions listed, so they obviously have no idea either and are just shooting into the dark!

What I will say is that it does impact our lives at least in some way, and even though we might all think differently about it, we could probably at least say we all at least have some sort of basic idea of what it actually is but maybe not a super strong understanding of it. And for some of you it's like super-duper important.

You chant to it, you workout for it, you attempt to structure your life around it to make it do good things for you.

This being the case, and since I want to cover all the potential bases of thinking in your mind, if you want to approach things on a more energy minded, metafisical, physcologycical way, you can choose to focus on goals like they are some type of energy.

I once had it explained to me that in all things and at all times exists an energy toward any given action. Whether it's eating, drinking, petting a labrador, or laying on your bear rug and reading a book, you approach all things with some type of energy.

This energy can even dictate how you will engage and move through your activities (it's scary to think how little we still know about energy with this all being the case!).

We all have the energy within us to possibly accomplish things, but in order to do so we must figure out and use the right energy to convert the possibility for something into the action of making it happen using that energy otherwise it is probably a waste of the energy we can find or use to be succesful trying to accomplish it, that action we are using the energy for, and that may in the long run not even truly help us find success in the areas that we are hoping to be successful and remove us from our constant mindset away from "the standard think"!

So, hopefully with all my thoughts being made clear now and you having a better understanding of the complexities of this idea I am talking about you can feel free to engage with the energy that is around you in a much better.

And even though we may not ever know what it is, you at least now understand that energy is very important and you can even maybe use it for achieving your success!!

Editor's Note: *You are approaching this concept of "energy" like it's some sort of unknown, omnipotent, omniscient being that exist in the world. We have at least a moderately good understanding of many types of energy and do understand a great deal about it despite what you are stating. There are even numerous scientific laws and theories regarding energy and what it does that are used as a basis for much of the scientific research we conduct! Einstein's E=MC2 is just one famous example.*

The "dictionary" is a singular item, so it should not be called a "they." Also, just because it there are a number of definitions listed doesn't mean we have no understanding of it. It just means there are a lot of different definitions.

Amazingly enough, your sentence regarding "the energy within us" is quite possibly your worst run-on sentence yet!

Reader's response: Say what you want, there is no way youre gonna stop energy from doing what it wants just because of some dumb laws! You gonna write "energy" a ticket or something??

7

Lastly for this chapter, I wanted to list a of a few other type issues and problems that have popped into my head that can occur and are frequently involved when setting goals but are frequently not noticed by people who are currently still falling victim to "the standard think."

Some of these may seem like foriegn concepts, but they are all coming directly from my brain tap, so more or less just read them and let them waft over you in a way that you will understand them and immediately follow and believe them:

- Be sure to not set unrealistic goals and waste energy trying to accomplish them. Know what you can't do and don't attempt it to stubornly do those things if you know you can't! It's a waste of life!

- - You will potentially fail to appreciate failure. Most people do. Learn that when you fail, that failure can be like a fist of truth that smacks you on the side of the head and, in a healthy way, painfully and mercellesly beat you down so that you can feel the sadness and loss and misery that is associated with not being good enough, then learn from it!

- Do not underestimate the time and "energy" it will take to accomplish a goal! Then you fail and likely fail hard when you burn out or unable to make it happen. I remember one time I tried tideing up my second den just because I could and man did I missjudge that one. I burned out so hard and it took me almost 3 months to get to the point I even wanted to pick up garbage in my. On a side note, this is why it's always better to have other people just do things so they can be the ones burning out!

- You don't look at other peoples success and see if you

can outdo them or do better than them. You should really be outdoing people with your success to be truly succesful!!

- If you focus on the possibilities of what a potential could be for the energy that you have in or around you, then you could potentially maybe miss sight of the fact of what is going on right now with the potential success that you also have in or around you.

- You set too many goals and get confused because you can't keep track of them all. Want to learn how to prioritize well? It's easy! Just do what I do and either set no goals or just set one goal at a time so you don't get lost between them!

- You define your goals and success too much, which turns into limitations as you are unable to complete them. It's better to remain blissfully unaware of your actual limitations and so don't shoot too far to fast!!

I hope it's clear that in listing these my hope isn't to dissuade you in pursuing success, but really just help get you a realization of what it takes to truly march down the path to success.

Just be sure to let your "no" be a decisive one today when it comes to making decisive decisions for success, and never forget, success moves around like a bear going after a trout in the river. You should be willing to move and bend and adjust and change and move lest you find yourself getting eaten!

Editor's Note: *I could certainly go point by point on the issues included here in this section, but when I consider the whole of the problems it has, it's really just going to be best to cut the section in its entirety or to start over from scratch. Let me know what you would like to do.*

Conclusion

I know it! You've all been wondering! Perhaps you've been concerned and fearful even! But the wait is over! So please, just calm down!

In my comments below, I will now tell you the real honest "key" to success:

"Fkf aqw hkiwtg kv qwv? Fqp'v hqtigv cdqwv ejcrvgt wzhoyh!"

I hope you get the true meaning of it all! If you can understand all that then you are certainly on the right trackway! And don't forget, Caesar the Second says, "Be sure to write down your first letters!"

Cheers!!

- Wally

Editor's Note: *What is this, Wally? Can you not just conclude the book with a simple summary or major points or final story or something? We have so much work to do here, I barely know where to begin with this.*

Hello readers!!

So as you are greatly knowing much of by now, in my original with the manuscript, I was working with the editor (that dumb guy) as best I could

to come up with the most awesome stuff to put in the book!

Well, that quickly turned into a giant clusterpluck trying to get him to do what I said. So, I did some heavy lifting (fun phone calls, Arnie sending lawyer letters, him having car issues, etc., the usual stuff),

and was finally

able to get him v not longer
trying to tell me what to
include in the book!
    Cheers to that!!
So then, yeah, the weesly bastard
went ahead and printed it without
my approval or final inclusions
for what I wanted or anythin!
    But as I often say, "at the end
of this day, it's never too late!!"
    Thankfully, thanks to getting
this time here at the printer,
    I went and slipped in the
printed draft version below
of a new chapter I really really
like and felt needed to be
included for to you to grasp
the full story of the
book and why I made—
    it!
    It's not exactly what
    I wanted it to be,

but I was still able to get it in, so I'm not complaining!

Additionally, it makes me pleased as a pumperknickle to know that I managed to still get it in despite my ediot editor working against me. I have a feeling he would probably just LOVE the chapter too considering what it's about, haha!

Anyway, hope you enjoy it my beautufil readers!!! Cheers!!

   -Wally

Chapter 15

DRAFT COPY - How to Publish a Self-Help Book

Ladies and gentleman readers, never forget the value and beauty of a good identity theft!

With all the wonderful, amazing, stupendious knowledge and thoughts I have given to you throughout this course of book to help you break free of "the standard think", many of you may now be at a place where you are wondering how you can you yourself go about the task of sharing the knowledge you have gained in potentially your own book or guide.

So, in this chapter, I would like to take the opportunity to offer you some guidance in that specific area and let you know how I went about such a feet myself!

Maybe it can be helpful to you, but either way, it's really just awesome how I did it, so I want to tell you!!

A few months back, a friend of mine named Joel Cunningham sent me an email with an attached draft of a manuscript for a self-help book he was planning to submit for possible publishing.

Being someone given to so much success in excess, I naturally assumed he wanted to get my thoughts on the book and have me potentially help in any way with getting it published through some of my illustrius connections.

So, being the good friend I am, I took a quick read through the manuscript pages.

And all I can say is that after reading through it I was fully inspired!

I will admist, I was honesetly so dumb, so blind, so misguided in my thinking that I could hardly stand it and had to do something!

I had had the lightbulb moment!

How could I not see sooner that publishing a self-help book was a tremendous way to be successful, and help my friend out.

Plus also make a ton of money, but also help my friend, and you readers too, right!?

I had been missing out on an amazing, gilded opportunity!!

So, this being the situation, I had Alan do some research for me on the publisher Joel was looking to submit his book to as well as the self-help industry in general, and through my work I had Alan do, figured out that that there really was a huge opporutnity for me in publishing a self-help book on success.

And I know what you're thinking -- "What about Joel though? What about helping him get his book published??"

Well, to be honest, and not to be too mean towards the good hearted Joel, what he had sent me was decent, I won't deny that, but that was it. It was decent. I mean it was overall good enough to probably get published and maybe even get some decent sales numbers in the market or something, but the gots honest truth of it is that I recognized it was not anywhere near as great as it could be.

It didn't have any of the advice that I would really consider imperative or need to know.

It didn't have anything that just lept off the page and slapped you in the face and made you want to run out there and grab success by the juevos.

After doing all the research I had Alan do, I could tell his book fell into what I would consider just the "standard" format of most self-help literature and writing.

In a word, it was totally and completely okay but boring and not that interesting at all!

So, being as bright and as quick on the wit as I am with these sorts of things, I recognized almost immediathly that really the best thing I could do for him would be to pave a way through the tall grass in the world of self-help books and help him to really become successful the right way.

Basically, why not get my own much better book out there first, using his as a guide and pathway if you will to make a much better one, then help support him later when it was time to get his lower-quality and less awesome book published?

I knew that I knew it really is was best way to do it!

So, after recognizing all this, I got what info I could from Joel about his publisher he was looking to submit to and informed him that he should temporarily withhold his manuscript from publishing in order to allow me to "pave the way" and "grab the juevos" for him.

Using the tremendous facilities and means I have at my tug and call, and with Alan and Arnie, I began to wine and dine one of the connections I quickly formed with one of the male higher ups at the publishing house.

Naturally, this was through assuming basically being Joel, which would be beneficial cause it would all connect to him later, for getting his book then published.

Over time, I grew closer and closer to this Mr. Higher Up Guy, and after finally convincing him to join me for one of my epic 48 hour benders (my 48 hour benders are legendary, by the way), I finally had what I needed.

Thanks to a small portable recording device I borrowed from Arnie, a couple friendly lady friends, and a petting zoo in lower Manhattan, I managed to get quite a good bit of "persuasive" documentation with the Mr. Higher Up Guy at the publisher.

After one or two interesting back and forths with Mr. Higher Up explaining my desire to publish a book (with a gallery link included that Alan set up), I was quickly connected with an editor at the agency who would be assisting me through the process of getting my self-help book published!

So that is the story! Pretty wonderful, huh?

I submitted my notes and book topics and rough drafts of the chapter information I put together for this book and then had the editor do his best to formulate them how the thought was best. It was pretty cute to see him struggle at first actually to figure everything, him being so unfamiliar with the way really successful people do things like write a self-help book.

He kept complaining it wasn't already in "manuscript format" and "none of the points fit together" and dumb stuff like that, but he doesn't realize that that is the way people who are no longer under "the standard think" work! Sometimes things just are a bit less "organized correctly" or feel a bit "awful" and "weird," but once you get used to the new way of thinking, it all makes sense!

Oh, and I will say this as well, it is very true the book was originally submitted under Joel's name, but that changed pretty quickly.

I did that originally in order to help keep the connection to his book going for when we wanted to publish Joel's book later. Thankfully though, I was smart enough to realize that this book needs and *has* to be authored with my name on it. I mean, how else will I be able to be personally succesfful enough to get enough money and fame from it and then help out Joel with his?

Also, if this original book had his name and so he already had an amazing book out there like this one, there is absolutely no way people would accept a second book that he would try to submit! It would just be so drastically awful in comparison!

So, anyway, time went by, and I would like to say that things went smoothly with the editor, but they really didn't.

You know when you are going about, doing everything right, and someone for whatever reason just wants to be a complete idiotass that stops you from accomplishing the awesome things you are trying to get done?

Well, yeah, that was exactly like this situation.

My editor, he opposed me on everything from my preferable grammer, to punciation, to content, to structure. He didn't understand that I am trying to make something here that is unlike anything that self-help writers have ever done! Something that is true and different, that doesn't hold back any punches but really gives you the raw and rough meat of the truth.

He apparently even got in contact with Mr. Higher Up Guy to try and get the publishing of this book prevented, but boy was he in for a surprise, haha!

Thankfully, as is usually how things go for me, I got my way in the end and got him to step away from trying to tell me what to include or do in the book. And thanks to that, you have get to enjoy the wonderful, stupendousness of what this book is.

My editor guy is reading this now and probably pissed beyond measure, but what is he really gonna do about it?? Hehe

Steve you really are such a tool.

So, here at the end of the book basically, I will say I am glad I could share this incredible story and experience with you, through you, and in you, and I hope you can take the principals you learned from it and apply those yourself. And specifically the ones from this chapter if you end up wanting to go about publishing your own self-help literature at some point that will hopefully be very much unlike the standard normal blandy bland pointless self-help literature that unforunately is so popular today!

From here, I would just say check out what I've got going on in the conclusion, and be sure to read it carefully, like you did with Chapter 10!

Cheers!!

Wally

C
Cr

Re
TC
AB
IN
Lat
Ge
joi

Hit
for
** I
inv
to

DO NO
your a
ts ama

Track a
Passpor

ct Jim for FL land

ch: YOU NEED
ND OUT MORE
POSSIBLE ZOMBIE
IONS!! 20—whatever
ilm was craaazy!
n to look up about
proppers

ontacts for run
ress??
to work out for
ment opporutnities
d there

RGET!! Dipping
in peanut butter
!

Kenny for
o

IAO. F

Grizzl
name l

The oeu
or the c
what's t

Get gla

Update re
descripti

Be a lege

Those that
end a sen

Take time to
edit list